From Vienna

ISABELLE KENAGY

To my great grandmother, Ilse Schlesinger Angove (Anigovsky).

Although this book is a testimonial, I could never write something that could describe how much I love you.

Thank you for being the sweetest person in my life and for making this entire book possible.

Your story will not be forgotten.

Chapter 1:

Ilse

Vienna

Winter 1938

February has been and always will be my favorite month. It is the perfect intersection of seasons. February in Vienna marks the beginning of the end of cold temperatures for the fashionable, not-so-weather-friendly Viennese. Mutti is still in the winter process of making trinkschokolade, but she no longer demands that George and I always wear our double-layered winter coats. The one thing that separates this month from all the others is that Helga takes us ice-skating, and it happens to be warm enough to show off my favorite dress.

Mutti first saw the dress in Frau Kaltenbach's window on Kohlmarkt. She had never taken me to get a dress fitted, especially not at Frau Kaltenbach's. I had walked up to Frau Kaltenbach's expecting to see another plain grey or plaid skirt and jacket like the ones Mutti always chose for me. Instead, the most glamorous dress stood in front of me. It had a blonde, spotted fur collar and cuff. It was made of dark purple velvet and flared out just so it fell at my mid-calf.

The dress is my most prized possession. It makes me feel less like the neighborhood's dear liebling and more like the fashionable Ilse

Schlesinger I so badly want to be. My older cousin Edith even commented on its elegance when I showed it to her a few weeks ago. Edith almost never compliments my wardrobe as hers is so colorful and exciting compared to my childish, bland one. Taking all my lack of glamour into consideration, I was bursting with anticipation for my dress' debut.

Helga threw open the door and gave a firm, "Miss Ilse! It is time to get out of bed and start our day!"

I didn't waste a moment throwing off my creme duvet as I knew today we were ice-skating.

"I'll be at breakfast in 20 minutes, Helga!" I yelled back.

"Ilse please don't scream across the house," replied Mutti as she waltzed into my room in her flowing dressing gown. "You know I don't appreciate when you yell. It wakes the neighbors, disrupts our house, and simply is not graceful."

Mutti knew the last reason would get to me. The street would be noisy in an hour and George would probably knock over a porcelain vase in 20 minutes, but Mutti knew I wanted to be graceful no matter what.

She slipped out of my room and danced into George's with a slight cheer in her voice. It was Friday, so she could open the store late and close early for the Sabbath. It was her day of what she called "secular relaxation." While I don't know what that means, it sounds sophisticated. I hear that word secular quite a lot when I listen to Papa's conversations with the smart men that stop by.

While George entertained Mutti I carefully unwrapped my beautiful dress and slipped it on. I stretched out my stockings until they almost fit; I was growing too fast for Mutti to buy me new stockings. I then double-checked the hallway and slid out my secret contraband.

Edith had bought it as a special Hanukkah present just for "her favorite younger cousin." I'm sure she had gotten our other younger cousin Miriam something as well, but she knew I liked to feel special. The small box held some powder, and light pink lipstick, and the slightest bit of rouge. I had never dared to wear the rouge but I liked to dab the lipstick and powder on when I needed to feel grown up and pretty. Today was one of those days.

After slipping on my shoes, grabbing my skates, and tucking my little box back in its secret place, I ran down the stairs to breakfast.

On the table there were three plates of eggs and toast, two cups of chocolate, and a cup of coffee for Mutti. Mutti appeared at the top of the staircase dressed in a form-fitting olive green skirt and jacket. Her hair was curled and pinned back and she wore a dark shade of red on her lips.

"Ilse! George! I'm leaving to meet your father at the store and keep everything in order. Be nice to Helga and have fun skating. Helga, make sure they don't do anything too rash," Mutti teased.

"As always, Miss Regine" responded Helga with a slight smile.

"I'll be home at 4 pm to start preparing for Shabbat. Helga, could you and the children pick up carrots and brisket? Now come here and give your mother a kiss goodbye."

George and I ran to give our mother her daily goodbye kiss. George and I were always competing for her attention. Papa would always love George more, but Mutti appeared to love everyone equally and George and I made it our personal goal to throw off that balance in favor of ourselves.

~

The walk down to the ice skating rink was lovely as always. George stole a roll of bread from the pantry and threw chunks at birds as we walked. I walked a few feet ahead of George and Helga and pretended I was a fashionable lady walking through the streets of Vienna without a pesky younger brother and an over-attentive maid.

"Ilse don't walk too far ahead," Helga commanded, ruining my daydream.

"I'm not far at all," I retorted.

"Ilse come feed these birds with me!" George yelled with delight.

I spun on my feet and with cold derision said, "George feeding the birds is for children, and I am not a child."

Helga was mere seconds away from a lecture on pleasantry and kindness when we arrived at the rink and George took off running. Shedding my illusions of glamour, I followed him gleefully.

The rink was filled with children from our neighborhood and from the Innere Stadt near the Hofburg. Some young couples were there enjoying the tolerable weather, while some older women looked on and indulged in nostalgia.

George and I skated for an hour while Helga observed us from a bench. Needing a sip of water, I wandered off the rink and recognized two brothers from my school: Franz and Rolf Schroeder. I looked behind them and saw poor, skinny Sigmund Goldstein cowering by a large linden tree. As I got closer I could make out what they were saying, and a mixture of fear and confusion filled my body.

"You ugly, disgusting Jew. I bet your mother is a whore and your father is a fiend. When my father and his party come to power you and the rest of your race will get what you deserve," shrieked Franz.

Sigmund sank to the ground as his eyes filled with tears.

Rolf jumped in and said, "Hitler is coming and then I won't have to lay my eyes on your filth.

How do you even go to my school? How do you have the money to live here? You stole it from us, that's how."

I stood there for a minute, my mind drawing a blank. Who is this Hitler? Why are they doing this?

Then George came rambling towards me and I knew in that instant that whatever they were saying was bad; George should not hear it. So, I pretended to trip. I stumbled, gave a cry for help, and landed right on Franz Schroeder giving Sigmund just enough time to get away.

"What the hell!?" exclaimed Franz.

"I am so sorry. I must have tripped on my skates," I said in the most kind and airy voice I could muster. Mutti may be a settled down Hausfrau, but she taught me the importance of using womanly power to weasel your way through difficult situations.

"Ilse? I'm so sorry I..." Franz trailed off. I knew he had always held a soft spot for me. He had shown interest in me before his father decided to hate Jews, and it seemed he couldn't entirely shake it from his mind.

"George, We're leaving now," I declared.

As Helga saw me walking back, she jumped up and followed me back to the apartment. Number 5 Hoher Markt was safe, I thought to myself. Mutti would be there getting Shabbat dinner ready, and Papa would read the paper and smoke his pipe. George would dart around trying to get attention, and I would finish my reading for school. After dinner, I would curl up next to Mutti and ask her questions about Franz and Rolf's words. She would tell me they were kind and mean nothing, and I would happily fall asleep.

Instead, as we rode the elevator up, I heard a congregation of male voices. We entered and I saw Papa sitting with three of his friends from synagogue. They ignored us as they focused intently on their argument. Papa's friend and Sigmund's father Mr. Goldstein were the loudest.

"I say Hitler or Schuschnigg, it doesn't matter. They both love fascism and hate Jews. We're damned either way," he thundered.

Papa countered, "Schuschnigg doesn't beat Jews in the streets. Hitler does. I have heard from

13

my friends in Berlin that the Nazis have begun to commend those who murder Jews."

"All of you stop it. There are children here and it's Shabbat. You need to go home to your wives who are no doubt slaving away over Shabbat dinner and enjoy your families. Goodnight," interrupted Mutti.

And with that the men left and Mutti and Papa acted like nothing had happened. I sat down at the dining room table feeling endless confusion and wondering what had happened to my little world.

Chapter 2:

Edith

Vienna

Winter 1938

Edith,

There is something I need to tell you. Meet me at
Demel's after lunch.

~Hans

The first thing that caught my eye that morning was this hastily written note. It was written on a tiny piece of crème card that Mutter must have left on my dresser while I was still sleeping. While the thought of Hans coming by late last night just to pass along this note made just the slightest smile appear on my face, I was still annoyed by his behavior the last time I had seen him. He had dismissed me as a childish young girl who knew nothing of love, life, work, or the world. He talked all night of his aspirations as a lawyer and future as a man of the world, but when I had brought up the prospect of being a writer, he had laughed and told me I would grow out of this silly aspiration when I was a little older.

He was rude and condescending, but I had it in my heart to forgive him. Still, Liesl and I were planning on discussing the whole situation over lunch today. Before any of that could happen, I had to help Mutter and do my daily, rather menial tasks.

First on the list was polishing the silver from last Shabbat. It seemed that by the time the last piece of silver was done being polished, the first one needed to be done all over again. On the one hand, silver was satisfying to clean as the metal would slowly reveal its beauty as the grime was wiped away. On the other hand, it was also the most disgusting with its mysterious combination of black and brown stains.

"Good morning Mutter," I said as I walked out of the hallway in my stockings and day dress.

"Good morning my dear. Did you sleep well? Ready to finish the silver?" She responded cheerfully.

"Of course, Mutter. I was hoping to be done with my chores by noon to meet Liesl and then Hans. Is that possible?"

"Yes, but would you mind picking up bread and vegetables for dinner on your way home?"

"Yes Mutter."

The polishing of silver tediously progressed into the late morning. Our maid Louisa came in and out periodically while she dusted and organized the house. She had been working for us for years as a nanny. While Mutter and I were plenty capable of doing chores on our own, we couldn't bear to let her go when I outgrew the need for a nanny. So, Louisa spent her days creating various tasks for herself and arbitrarily rearranging the tchotchkes.

Around 11:30, Mutter and I were finished with our main chores, or at least the ones she needed my help with. That left me some time to freshen up and look presentable for Hans. I chose a grey suit, a fur coat, and a red lipstick that left me feeling sophisticated and less like the young girl Hans had made me out to be.

~

To make sure I didn't miss Hans, I met Liesl at Demel's. It was the premier dessert maker in Vienna and their coffee was marginally acceptable. My family had always enjoyed this place and my younger cousins, Ilse, Miriam, and George, often came here with their parents for birthdays or other special occasions. Demel's had also been one of my main meeting places with Liesl. Since we first bumped into each other on the streetcar when I was a younger student and she was almost graduated, we had formed an unlikely friendship based on our shared love for gossip and the finer things in life.

"Hello. May I please get a table for two?" I asked the waiter at the front.

"Of course ma'am. Follow me."

Just then Liesl fell into the room in a flurry of packages, fabrics, and jewelry.

"Darling Edith! I'm here and only a minute late!" Liesl cried.

We followed the waiter to our table as fellow patrons observed Liesl's unrestrained style and almost gaudy display of jewels. I knew they were mostly fake or cheap Czech crystal, but these curious on-lookers only saw the velvet, gold, and silver that draped over Liesl and made her the most fascinating person in the room.

"So dear Edith, how's it going with that adorable boyfriend of yours? You two have been together for less than a year and yet *this man* has invaded all of our conversations," Liesl remarked as she settled into her chair

I shared with her Hans's rude comments and my conflicting emotions. Of course, Liesl responded with a dismissive, "Men are fragile creatures. They like to think they are in charge and when a woman seems to have a single genuine thought, they attack to protect their delicate personas." She told me there was no reason to be mad at Hans. She advised me to enjoy whatever he had planned for the afternoon and not to worry about his immature outburst.

After inhaling a sacher torte and coffee Liesl said, "Well Edith I must get going. I am going to try and find a job this afternoon. I am really quite done living off of generous men who wish to woo me. This afternoon I will become a real independent woman who can buy her own jewelry." Under her breath she added, "That is, if I can find employment at all."

"Liesl! I'll try and come by for coffee tomorrow or the next day. Good luck with your ambitious endeavors," I teased.

As Liesl left, I saw Hans walk in the door and spot me immediately. He was handsomely dressed in a coat and tie and had a gentlemanly sway in his step. He exchanged quick pleasantries with Liesl and then let his eyes land on me again. I tried to hide the smile on my face but it was becoming increasingly more difficult. I felt like the most glamorous woman in the world. First a lavishly dressed woman comes to see me and next a slick and handsome young man. The thought made me blush as I felt I was playing a character.

"How are you Edith? I'm sorry I was such a fool," He said as he hung his coat on the side of the chair.

"I'm perfectly fine. And yes, you were rude but I've put it behind me," I responded confidently.

"I'm glad we're past it so I can tell you my news. My father has offered me a full time position at his law firm and has given me my first real case. He said he wants to train me and has told me I'll inherit the firm when he retires. Father's so old it seems it could be soon!" Hans spilled excitedly.

"Oh I'm so happy for you Hans," I replied with forced enthusiasm. I was truly happy for Hans but it only made me feel more like a little girl with no real prospects in life. I had always hoped I would marry Hans eventually, but the thought began to cross my mind that he would never marry me if his success continued to grow. I may have been getting ahead of myself as marriage was still at least four years in the future, but nevertheless it frightened and depressed me.

Hans was never the one to notice subtleties such as the way I failed to meet his eyes, so he continued talking about his future with great passion and excitement until he jumped up and said, "Edith I want to take you somewhere. You'll love it, I just know it!"

We walked out of Demel's, crossed through the gates of the Hofburg, walked through the gardens, and eventually arrived at a grand statue of Maria Theresa. I was beginning to wonder why we had come to greet the grandiose statue of this ancient empress when Hans spun me around and pointed up.

"There," he said. "It is the Kunsthistorisches. They house paintings from Caravaggio, Velazquez, and even modernists like Klimt. I was dismissive of your passions and I thought I'd make it up to you."

"Hans, this is incredible! I had heard of this museum but I have never had the opportunity to visit. Do they really have works by Caravaggio?"

"Yes and they have some of your favorite landscapes."

I squealed with delight and entered the ornate building. Large staircases flanked the room as Egyptian art greeted me on one side while the antiquities greeted me from the other. European paintings sat right in front of me beckoning me to dive in.

~

As Hans and I exited the building, he gave me the most endearing look. He smiled and said, "Edith, I hope you enjoyed today. You mean the world to me and I do look forward to the adventures we have in the future, especially once I have money."

I swung around to face him and said, "Thank you for today Hans. I would love to stay later and enjoy the rest of the afternoon, but I must get home to Mutter. Will I see you tomorrow?"

"I'll do everything in my power to make sure you do."

And with that he gave me a quick kiss on the cheek and we parted ways. I walked back to our neighborhood near Judenplatz to pick up bread from Mr. Wilensky and carrots from the fresh market.

While walking through my beautiful city, I began to think fondly of Hans. I began thinking about our lives in the future, the amount of children we would have and the meals I would make for my family. I thought about where we could have our wedding. Mutter would insist on the synagogue but we could have a fabulous party after.

I was beginning to get lost in visions of our future when I realized how far away that was. First I wanted to paint, write, and read all the great works. Hans had more schooling to do and money to make. Maybe we would never even get married. Regardless it was far in the future. It was nothing to concern myself with at 17.

Chapter 3:

Miriam

Vienna

Winter 1938

My feet hit the cobblestones hard as I ran after Rachel. Our family was having Rachel's family over for dinner and we had promised to pick up fish for our mothers. The moment we left Rachel called out, "Let's race! 1, 2, 3…" and took off before she had said go.

We were at least four or five kilometers from the center of town, but we could still hear the church bells that sat nestled deep inside Vienna's folds strike 6pm. I kept running.

I had never been particularly fit. My cousin Ilse was swift, agile, and strong and my other cousin Edith was a fantastic swimmer. I, on the other hand, did not inherit these athletic traits from the Schlesingers. Instead, I received my mother's stout Russian figure that was meant for surviving Siberian winters, not racing through the streets of Vienna. Rachel was lucky. Her parents were tall and slim, almost Aryan in appearance. Consequently, Rachel was the most athletic girl in our class. She could even beat some of the boys in a sprint. Our teacher would say to us, "You girls are the perfect best friends. You are both quick: Miriam intellectually and Rachel physically."

Our teacher wasn't wrong. I learned to read before anyone else in my class. I spell words better than my parents and I can tell you all the multiplication tables up to 20. I help Rachel with her homework and she makes sure no one makes fun of me when I can't run as fast as the others or can't lift a bucket of water.

When Rachel reached the shop, I was still about 50 meters behind, panting heavily, and starting to slow to a walk because I lacked the motivation to run any further. I cried out, "Why do we always have to run everywhere? It hurts and makes me sweaty. Plus, you always win so there is no game."

"Miriam, running is fun! Don't you like the feeling when it's cold and your cheeks and nose start to get red? And I don't always win. I remember you won once."

"Rachel that was two years ago. We were 9!"

We approached the fish shop and were greeted with Ms. Aaron's typical, "Girls, girls, girls! You must be here for your mothers! Are you dining together? Oh, I just love the idea of that!"

Rachel responded, "Yes Ms. Aaron... we need two large trouts... and you're welcome to come tonight. We're having Rachel's family over but I'm sure my mother would love to have you as well."

"Well I'll talk to Mr. Aaron and we might be able to make an appearance," Ms. Aaron said with a smile.

Rachel and I walked back to our block giggling about Ms. Aaron's squeaky voice and Mr. Aaron's funny mustache. We delivered the trout to our mothers and sat on our stools listening to the men of the community talk about important grown-people things.

"The Austrian economy is doing worse and worse each year. It's the same for Germany! I hate Hitler as much as the next but I can't blame our gentile neighbors for seeing the positives in him. He could just be a lot of talk. He might not hurt us all that bad," my father thundered.

"Joseph how can you say that? I heard they have a prison camp called Dachau just for leftists and Jews. I doubt it is the equivalent of your brother's ski resort in Salzburg," Rachel's father said with a burst of deep laughter.

Our elderly neighbor added, "I see Joseph's point. This is Austria. We aren't Germans and the whole country knows it. I know Schuschnigg is a fool, but he is an Austrian. All these talks with

Hitler will only amount to an alliance. Schuschnigg has too much Austrian pride to allow for annexation."

Mother announced dinner and the entire group moved swiftly to the table. The night was filled with laughter and fish and matzo-ball soup. The men talked of their new favorite cigar brand and the local economy while the women talked about expensive gifts they wished they had. Mother talked all about my Aunt Regine's collection of perfumes from Paris and her silk scarves from her sister's store in Paris, Hermes. Mother added rather strangely, "That woman may be a sell-out, but she has a wonderful wardrobe. Regardless, the two other wives of this family couldn't care less about their Jewish heritage. They just want to join the Viennese upper class."

After our mother deemed it "bedtime," Rachel and I curled up in my bed while the mothers gossiped and the fathers had their late night smoke. Eventually we fell asleep to the sounds of my father's booming voice singing "Wien, Wien nur du allein."

~

My father and I walked along the Ringstrasse while he told me of all the games he used to play as a boy. He told me his brothers would race around the Ringstrasse trying their best to avoid colliding with the crowds of people. He told me how they would kick a ball around Stadtpark until they hit an unsuspecting pedestrian and once they tried to swim in the Danube in the middle of the day. We laughed as we hurried to catch the streetcar. My father picked me up and put me on the deck and then jumped to catch the rail just as the streetcar was leaving.

We were headed into Vienna for two reasons. I was going to visit with my cousins, Ilse, George, and Edith, and father was going to work. He worked right next to Uncle Berthold and Aunt Regine in a little shoe store. He sold all sorts of shoes. He had brown leather ones with heels for the ladies and stained black leather oxfords for the men. He had also started experimenting with canvas shoes for children. I loved watching my father work when Ilse and Edith were too busy to play. Ilse went to a much fancier school than I did so she was always busy with school work and Edith was all grown up and had too many friends to spend time with me.

Today, however, we had arranged a specific time for the three of us to see each other. George was invited but he was a boy so no one wanted him to come and he didn't really want to either.

We approached Hoher Markt and my father gave me a kiss on the forehead and said, "Go on now. It's number 5 on the top floor. I'll see you when you're done. I'll be in the store."

I absolutely loved going to Ilse's because I got to take the elevator all the way to the top floor. We didn't have any elevators in our neighborhood but Ilse told me almost all her friends have them.

I got to the top door and rang the bell. Helga answered, "Oh Miss Miriam you're here! Miss Ilse, Miss Edith, Miss Miriam is here."

Ilse and Edith came out from the dining room and greeted me with two large hugs. Edith gave me a very motherly hug that clearly said, "Dear child I'm so glad you got here safe," while Ilse gave me the hug of a best friend that said more, "I was dying of boredom until you got here so thank god you've finally arrived!"

Edith spoke first, "Miriam how do you feel about walking around the neighborhood? Ilse says it's boring but you never get to see this area of the city so I thought you might like it."

I responded quietly, "I like the first district, so that's great."

"Perfect, it's settled!"

Edith walked away to grab her coat while Ilse pulled me aside and started chatting in my ear, "How is Rachel? I heard she fell into the Danube while trying to show Adolf she could jump over the whole river."

Rachel was famous for her crazy antics but that wasn't completely true. I told Ilse, "She didn't quite 'fall in.' She pretended like she was going to jump and then tripped and landed in the mud."

Ilse let out a squeal of laughter and began telling me all about her school friends and everything that had happened since we last saw each other. Edith arrived with the coats and some bread for the walk and interrupted our conversation with a, "Miriam, Ilse! Let's go... Bye Helga! Have fun with George!"

While we walked through the city Ilse and I exchanged a storm of teenage gossip while occasionally pausing to ask Edith something about her much more sophisticated life. Most of our questions were about her boyfriend Hans. Whenever we probed about their relationship, she would give us a vague answer and then Ilse, and I would go back to dreaming about our own future boyfriends and beautiful weddings in the middle of the city. We shared friends and knew some of the people at each others' school, so we would gossip about them incessantly.

The day went on like that until we had made full circle and arrived back at Hoher Markt. Ilse and I gave each other suffocating hugs and laughed as George pressed his face against the window to look down at us. Edith gave both of us a fashionable kiss on both cheeks and then left with the excuse of needing to pick up a dress. Ilse went back up the elevator and I walked back to my father's shop.

Chapter 4:

Ilse

Vienna

Spring 1938

The slamming of boots echoed through our
apartment; the radio screamed in the corner; Mutti
paced through the apartment spitting out expletives;
the building shook; the windows vibrated; voices

cheered from the street. The Nazis had come to Vienna.

At least, that's what the radio said. Mutti and Papa said nothing about what was going on. They just grumbled to themselves as Papa rubbed his temples and Mutti fidgeted with her bracelet. They said nothing of Hitler thinking somehow I wouldn't know who the man was if they didn't tell me.

They were wrong. I knew about Hitler. My classmates talked about his master race and Third Reich and brilliant plans for the future. I knew he didn't like Jews and I found the Nazis to be brutish and scary. That was all I knew, but it was enough to know what was going on. I could see the bright red arm bands as they flashed by the window on the street below. I saw a man paint a swastika on a wall and another throw his hand into the air like a blade. The scene was strangely enchanting. I pressed my face up to the cold glass until my nose was all squished up like a pig.

"Ilse, get away from there right now! Why don't you practice your violin?" Mutti shrieked as she grabbed my arm.

"Mama, don't you see all the men down there? Can't we go out and watch the parade?" I pleaded with obvious curiosity.

George popped up from his chair as chanted, "Oooh Parade! Parade! Parade!"

"Ilse, you don't understand those men are not exciting. They are..." she trailed off nervously only to pick up with a confident and abrupt, "This day is just like any other and we will treat it so."

She led George and me to the door and told Papa to go to the store. She gave Helga specific directions to not let anyone into the apartment. With that, she took both George and my hands and led us out to go grocery shopping. As we got into the elevator the voices and boots only got louder and louder. The elevator started to rattle with the sounds of men's voices and women's cheers.

The second we got out, a wave of energy slapped me across the face. People were crowded up against each other saluting the swastika and shouting unintelligible things. Women were waving handkerchiefs and blowing kisses. The marching men looked like they were about to fight a war but I did not know what war. In fact, Mutti says there

36

will be no more wars. She said there already was a war to end all wars and it ended a long time ago.

Mutti clenched our hands hard until George started to squirm and complain. She then led us straight through the crowd until the pack of marching soldiers prevented her from crossing the street. While we waited for a gap in the line of men, I looked around. I saw a man draw a Jewish star on the pavement only to scribble a large X over it. I heard a woman's shrill voice complain about the Jewish problem.

George pointed and shouted, "Hey there's Papa's friend from synagogue--"

Mutti cupped her hand over his face and said very calmly, "George, please do not say a word until we are at the store."

"Yes Mutti."

I began to understand the reason for Mutti's tense behavior. I started to realize the dark meaning of everything I was hearing and seeing. This excitement was no longer excitement to me. It was simply a mob. They hated the Jews, me and my family. We could no longer be Jewish in the streets. We were to be Jewish only with the people who knew us well. This Hitler did not want us around but if we stayed very quiet, maybe he wouldn't notice that we were even here in the first place.

We arrived at the bakery where Frau Wilensky greeted us with a hasty and worried sales pitch. About halfway through her explanation of their freshest bread, she broke and told us to come to the back of the shop immediately.

"Come on, come on! I don't like to be in the storefront and you most certainly should not be on the streets. What were you thinking Regine?" Frau Wilensky asked hurriedly.

"I know I shouldn't have left, but I didn't expect the ferocity of the crowd and I thought acting normal was the best course of action." Mutti responded with guilt in her voice.

"Well we can't go back in time so you might as well stay with me and Jacob until the action dies down. Come, I have some tea in the living room." Frau Wilensky responded.

We followed her into the back and huddled together for hours, exchanging brief comments and worried looks. We waited: me in fear, Mutti in guilt, and George in blissful ignorance.

Chapter 5:

Edith

Vienna

Spring 1938

I was up and out the door before anyone had
opened their eyes. I was nervous for what was going
to happen. I barely left myself time to think about
what I was doing. I just knew I had to leave before

anyone was awake because Mutter would never let me leave the house.

Today was the day the papers had talked about for weeks. Hitler was marching into Vienna. I had been following his journey through Austria from Munich in the hopes that he wouldn't ever reach Vienna.

But, today he had done it, dashing all my hopes for Vienna's safety. As I stood in the doorway putting on my coat, Hitler was crossing the city boundary and laying siege to my hometown.

I knew this meant the beginning of the end for my family. My mother denied the danger posed by the Nazis and remained steadfast in her positivity about Austrian politics, no matter who was in charge. My father was aware but scared and chose to actively ignore the political articles in the papers. I was terrified but also fascinated. That is why I was going to the speech today. I knew it was dangerous and some might say it would be wrong to attend, but I had to see this horrible creature for myself and I had to know what I was up against.

I walked out on the street in hopes of seeing recognizable faces from our neighborhood. I was desperate for some familiar faces. However, masses were already starting to build up on the streets in front of me and the faces I might have recognized were overwhelmed by all the faces I had never seen before.

I walked down along Bauernmarkt to Heldenplatz to try and find the perfect spot. I wanted to be far away enough to be unnoticed, but close enough that I could see Hitler and his henchmen. Hitler was due to start speaking in an hour. So I waited.

~

When Hitler's car entered the square, a roar began to rise up from the crowd as people took notice of the dark-haired man with a tiny moustache. Shouts of "Heil!" were raised and people began surging forward. It was fanfare I had only ever seen American movie stars receive.

The car pulled to a stop and I saw him get out and stand up. After seeing so many images of this domineering, masculine figure, I was surprised to see such an average-looking man. He appeared awkward, like an old king who was once a great war hero and is now the laughing stock of his country. How could such an unimpressive thing command such a frightful regime?

Hitler approached the podium and the crowd pulsed once more with incredible excitement. A little blond girl next to me squealed and began to jump up and down yelling a fierce, "Heil Hitler!' with every jump. Her mother squeezed her cheek and gave her the most endearing look. I was barely able to hide my absolute disgust only to avoid unwanted attention.

Hitler began to speak and his first words were barely audible as the crowd began to scream. It was a noise louder than any I'd ever heard before. I knew it was a scream of adoration, but to me it seemed like one of horror. The crowd calmed down and I began to hear what he was saying.

"I myself, as Führer and Chancellor of the German people, will be pleased to enter Austria, my homeland, once again as a German and a free citizen. But the world must convince itself that the German people in Austria have been seized by a soulful joy, and see that their rescuing brothers have come to their aid in their hour of great need. Long

live the National Socialist German Reich! Long live
National Socialist German Austria!"

His voice echoed through the square
bouncing off of buildings and causing the crowd to
roar in approval. A horrible shiver passed through
my body. I didn't know how I would do it, and I
knew my parents would have to be persuaded, but I
needed to get out of this country. Immediately.

Chapter 6:

Miriam

Vienna

Spring 1938

It was 5 in the morning when I began to hear screaming. My mother ran into my room in her dressing gown with a panicked expression.

"Mama what is happening? Why is it so loud?" I yelled at her.

"Darling there are soldiers marching into town today and it has...excited some of our neighbors," she replied with feigned confidence.

The sounds from outside seemed to turn back and forth between horror and applause and the noise only got louder as boots began to hit the ground. Car motors grumbled and horns honked as Mama encouraged me to go back to sleep.

I protested loudly, "Mama I can't even talk to you without screaming let alone go to sleep!"

Mama nodded her head and brought me to the kitchen saying, "Sit down dear and I'll make you some breakfast. Would you like milk?"

Papa entered the room while Mama was leading me through the breakfast options and stood there deep in thought. I interrupted Mama with a loud, "Papa why is the army marching into the city? I've never even seen the army before."

Papa responded, "Miriam, these are not our soldiers. They are German soldiers."

"Why are the Germans here? I thought they had their own country. Why are they here?"

"Miriam there are things you don't yet understand, but I need you to stay inside today and try and ignore these soldiers. How about we draw together? I know you love doing that."

This proposal from my father was rather surprising. I hadn't drawn in at least a couple months and my father worked so hard that he rarely ever had time to spend with me let alone draw with me. I accepted his request. It was a Saturday after all. He wasn't supposed to work on the Sabbath. The thought of the Sabbath brought up a new question for me: aren't I supposed to go to synagogue in the morning for services? How are we going to be able to hear anything through this noise and why hasn't Mama started nagging me about what I'm going to wear? I don't have a lot of fancy clothes, but Mama always makes a fuss about looking nice for synagogue.

"Mama, am I going to synagogue this morning?" I asked quietly.

"No, Miriam. I think today we will stay inside and take a well-deserved rest. How does that sound? Now go on and draw with your father. You know he has such skill with art."

She did have a point. Papa was a brilliant artist. His drawings were always so precise. He told me he had learned to draw as a boy and had always kept the skill in his back pocket. As happy as I was to draw with Papa, my head was hurting so badly from the horrible noises outside. Our house obviously didn't have thick walls and everything was vibrating. I began to hear a noise that sounded like a very loud and grumbling car. There was some strange metal clacking and a crushing sound following that. My whole family seemed to have heard it as Mama went to the window. She looked out and gasped saying, "Joseph, they have tanks!"

"Mama what are tanks?" I asked with genuine curiosity.

She responded, "Large cars with guns attached," and muttered under her breath, "Completely unnecessary for a peaceful city."

As she was finishing her sentence there was a loud knock on the door. For a moment both Mama and Papa had obvious looks of panic covering their faces. As Papa opened the door he was relieved to see our rabbi standing there with his wife.

"Joseph, Berta, Miriam! I am here to say my goodbyes to all three of you. My wife and I had been planning on leaving for a while. We are leaving today and I encourage you three to leave as soon as possible. Who knows when you no longer will be able to," our rabbi said with a surprisingly calm tone.

My mother, shocked by news, asked him, "Where on earth will you go?"

"We have friends in England who are willing to help us and any other Jews fleeing Austria. When we get there we will try to bring more of you to England."

"Safe travels rabbi. We are sad to see you go."

"Berta I am asking you to do me a favor. There are so many of us here who will need help in the coming months. Please help your neighbors and stay close to one another. I will send word as soon as I'm able."

With that, the rabbi and his wife left and Mama and Papa stared off into space. I had never thought of leaving Vienna until the rabbi had mentioned going to England. I had always assumed I'd stay here forever. Then again, I kind of wanted to see England. I really wanted to see America. I heard everything there is beautiful and that everyone in America is rich. Maybe leaving Vienna wouldn't be so bad after all. I'm sure Mama and

Papa wouldn't mind. It would be quite the adventure and maybe I'd get some sleep without hearing all these loud soldiers.

Chapter 7:

Ilse

Vienna

Spring 1938

"The German national anthem follows a very clear tune and the words are easy to remember," said Frau Schneider as she passed out the lyrics of the German national anthem to the class.

"Ok everyone get ready in 1, 2…" She continued.

I started to stand confused at this sudden change in song when my teacher abruptly stated, "No, no, no. All Jews stay sitting. You do not sing the anthem."

For a moment I stood there completely bewildered. I knew that I couldn't be Jewish in the streets, but this wasn't the streets. This was my school. I spent almost every day here. Frau Schneider had been complimenting my writing and reading skills for years. I always thought I was one of her favorite pupils. Now, she won't even let me sing.

"Ilse, you are a Jew if I'm not mistaken. Sit down."

Her remark snapped me back into reality and I sunk into my chair pondering the strangeness of the whole situation. The rest of the class began to sing this new national anthem. It sounded like a bunch of coughing frogs. It was not a beautiful song. Nowhere near it. It was ugly and stupid and mean just like the Germans.

"Ok class, that was beautiful!" Frau Schneider said after the chorus of coughing frogs ended. "Let's take out our history book and find the page on Kanzler Bismarck. We must catch up on our new country's history!"

Several boys including Franz Schroeder let out a hoot at the mention of our "new country." I was fed up with all this Germany business.

~

At lunchtime I wandered over to Mathilde and our friends. Mathilde had been my closest friend since I started school. She had long blonde hair that she always wore in braids with little red ribbons at the bottom. She had the bluest eyes and was taller and more beautiful than all the other girls in our grade. We had a special spot in the schoolyard where we would sit together each day and have lunch with a small group of girl friends. Our daily ritual was to chat about the cutest boys and which girl was wearing the best dress and so on. Every once in a while Mathilde would teach us how to braid our hair like hers and we would while away our lunchtime braiding each other's hair. There had not been a day since we started Kindergarten that I had not sat next to Mathilde and our friends.

"Mathilde! Mathilde!" I called out. She glanced at me and turned her back. That was strange. I continued walking toward her as I started to ramble off all the things that had happened over the weekend. Her back was still turned. I started to get annoyed. "Mathilde!" I yelled as I stomped my foot hard against the pavement.

She spun around with a violent fire in her eyes and shouted, "What's wrong, Ilse?!"

"Why are you ignoring me? Let's go have lunch where we always do."

"Ilse we can't be friends anymore. You are a Jew. Soon you'll be gone to another school and I won't be able to see you...I can't see you." She still had anger in her voice but as she trailed off I saw a flicker of sadness in her eyes. In an instant the anger returned as she proclaimed, "I don't want to see you. You're a Jew." She spun back around and walked away as the rest of our friends waddled after her like ducklings following their mother. Not a single friend stayed with me. No one gave me a look of pity or remorse. They all just mimicked Mathilde's cold gaze and left.

I didn't understand how this could happen. Mathilde had been my best friend for years but with the stomp of a Nazi boot, she was gone. Because of that stupid red and black flag I was alone. I lost my best friend, my teacher, my neighborhood, and according to Mathilde, I was going to lose my entire school. I didn't understand how one man with a tiny mustache could make everyone in my life hate me. I wanted to scream. I wanted to go kick a Nazi in the shin and tell him to go back to Berlin. I especially wanted to go slap Mathilde across the face and tell her to snap out of it.

But I couldn't do any of that. Instead, I sat under a tree and ate my lunch alone. I felt my face get all scrunched up and tight and felt tears prick my eyes until they started to well up. Then one by one they rolled down my cheeks staining my brown paper bag lunch.

~

"Ilse, let's goooo!!" George said as I packed up my things. He seemed angry. I was angry. School had just ended and George was understandably itching to get home. I was too.

"Ilse, why is being a Jew bad?" George asked abruptly as we walked away from school.

"Because a few ignorant people said so." I responded a little impatient because if I was being entirely honest, I didn't even know the answer either.

George peppered me with questions: "Ilse, did you sing the German national anthem today? Did your friends ignore you too? Do we live in Germany now?"

On any normal day I would have rolled my eyes and told him to go away, but today I felt bad for him. I felt bad for me.

"George, I know today was strange but we are still in Austria. This is still our home and we still have our family. Our friends will come back to us soon enough, they're just mad right now." I told him with all the empathy I could muster.

His face started to drop and he looked as scared as a small child who had lost his mother in a crowd. For as annoying as my little brother was, I hated to see him on the brink of tears, so I told him, "George, everything is going to be fine. Mutti says it will be fine, and we know Mutti is always right."

With the mention of Mutti his face lit up and he seemed to forget about our school troubles. As we stood in the elevator I tried to forget too.

We opened the door to the apartment and heard a fit of laughter coming from the kitchen. George took off to see what caused it and called me over. I went into the kitchen completely dumbfounded by the stark contrast with the world outside and saw Mutti with an entire apple strudel laid out on the table, without a tablecloth.

To make apple strudel you need to lay a tablecloth over the table and then put the dough on top of that so you can roll up the dough at the end. Mutti had forgotten the tablecloth so now she had an entire apple strudel but no way to roll it up. Mutti, Helga, and George were all now dying of laughter because of the fatal mistake. I was simply curious about one thing: why was Mutti making an apple strudel in the middle of a Monday afternoon?

"Edith is getting married!" Mutti announced happily.

"What?" George and I said in unison.

"She is getting married to that lovely boy um… Hans? Yes! Hans is his name! They are getting married at the synagogue in three weeks and so I thought I'd make this apple strudel to celebrate their engagement," Mutti said excitedly.

At that moment Papa walked in and began ranting, "Why is that girl getting married? She's too young! Does she even know this boy?"

Mutti responded with frustration, "You know why she's getting married Berthold. Don't play dumb. It's what's happening, so now we will celebrate."

A wedding! My own cousin's wedding! Miriam and I had teased Edith about marrying Hans, but I never thought it would actually happen and happen so soon.

Chapter 8:

Edith

Vienna

Summer 1938

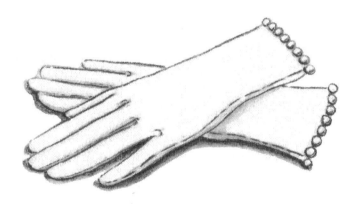

I'm getting married. I am actually about to walk down an aisle and marry Hans. In less than a half an hour I will be Mrs. Edith Rosenberg.

I thought this to myself while staring at my lovely white gown. It was my mother's wedding dress and it was wonderfully old-fashioned and tasteful. It had long sleeves with a lace trim and a straight skirt. I had a pair of heeled white shoes and beaded white gloves to go along with it. Each aspect of my wedding ensemble had such intricate details from the silver threads woven through my lace sleeves to the tiny pearl beads sewn into the trim of my gloves.

Sitting there in my slip and eyeing my pure white garments I began to get chills. How did this all happen so fast? Everything from the proposal to our engagement to the wedding planning had been rushed. Hans hadn't even proposed. Our parents had a conversation one night at dinner and right there at the table Hans' father suggested I marry Hans. I didn't even answer. It was just decided. We had reason, of course. Hans' family had a cousin in Australia who could get a visa for the Rosenberg family. To go with them, I had to be a part of the Rosenberg family.

Once our parents had decided on our marriage, everything was quickly set into motion. The synagogue was immediately notified. I had Mutter's dress brought in to fit my waist, and the menu was all set. I offered my opinion, but almost everything was decided by my mother. In the midst of this rushed wedding planning I barely had time to talk to Hans about the fact that we were getting married. We were about to promise to spend our entire lives together. The thought was too enormous for my 17 year-old brain to comprehend. I truly loved him and I was excited to marry him, but this was much different situation than anything I had ever imagined.

As I was combing through my thoughts, Mutter came in and began to talk up a storm. "Edith! We must get you dressed immediately. And look at that hair! Oy vey! I guess I'll just fix it right now."

"Mutter we have time. Calm down," I begged.

She began dressing me, sighing as she worked. Her hands worked through my hair at an amazing speed and, with an impressively delicate touch, she slipped the wedding dress over my head and onto my body. I was going to miss her dearly. "Mutter, I'm… um," I stammered.

"Don't say you're scared, Edith," she responded with a firm tone I wouldn't dare counter.

"Every woman is scared on her wedding day and to say it out loud does not make anything better. This may be rushed and you may be young, but you and Hans will be happy. I'm sure of it," she continued.

"But Muter, when we leave for Australia, what is going to happen? Will I see you again?" I asked, desperately trying to contain myself.

"Edith, you are a brave girl. You are my daughter. When you leave for Australia you will have a wonderful new life and I plan to join you as soon as I can. But please, don't focus on that. We have time. Focus on walking down the aisle."

With that she marched me out of my dressing room and towards the main chamber of the synagogue. As we were leaving I caught a glance of myself in the mirror. I looked like a bride. A grown-up woman marrying the man she loved. I appeared elegant and mature. The lace looked wonderful against my pale skin and the pearls shone brilliantly on my neck. I was prepared for this, no matter what the circumstance was.

Papa hooked his arm into mine as the music began to play. I inhaled the smell of the synagogue I had grown up in. I could smell my father's cologne and the treatment on the wood benches. I heard the violin whine and my cousins Ilse and Miriam giggling. I heard a cough or two and smelled the wax of the candle burning next to me. I looked up at the gorgeous blue and gold painted ceiling that had dazzled me as a little girl. We began to walk.

I looked up at Hans but turned away because I was blushing too hard. A bright red face against a clean white dress was not a flattering look. I spotted Liesl looking as beautiful and dramatic as ever as she inspected my dress and then gave me a nod of approval. Ilse and Miriam were right in front of her gazing at me with adoration and awe. Mutter was in the front row and showed the smallest smile which finally gave me the confidence to glance back at Hans again. He looked so handsome. He wore a perfectly tailored suit and a black silk Yakama with silver trim. His shoes were shined so well that they acted like a crystal ball and reflected light into every direction.

I finally reached the front and stood next to Hans. The rabbi was talking but I could not tell you what he was saying. All my attention was on Hans. His eyes were looking right into mine and I began to smile until I was smiling so hard my cheeks felt like they were going to burst. Hans gave me a nod and then walked forward and smashed the traditional wine glass. I was doing everything I could to hold back my tears of joy when Hans put his arm against my back and pulled me in for the lightest, most appropriate kiss. I figured the ceremony must have been over because the congregation stood up and began to cheer. I began to laugh with pure joy and clapped with delight. Ilse and Miriam immediately rushed up to give me a hug and I bent down to greet them. Hans and I walked hand-in-hand out of the synagogue as husband and wife. I had a new life and in that moment, walking next to my dearest Hans, I could feel everything coming together.

~

I had changed into a shorter dress to allow for dancing and a less formal occasion. It was light blue and had a fuller skirt that puffed out when I twirled. I kept my white heels, dabbed on a little red lipstick, and felt ready to greet my family and friends as a new wife. Hans' mother and father had hosted a dinner with a small group after the ceremony, and now a larger group was coming by the house for a night of dancing and celebrating. I walked out into the party that was already starting to grow and saw Liesl walking up the stairs. She had, for my sake, kept her outfit more demure and wore a tight-fitting maroon dress with only one strand of fake diamonds. Hans was in the other corner wearing a relaxed suit. The moment he saw me, a smile began to creep onto his lips. He walked over to me, wrapped his arm around my waist, and gave me a stronger kiss than the one at the synagogue. Mutter would most certainly find it inappropriate, but, to my surprise, I enjoyed it. He held me there for a moment until he let me go and said in the quietest voice, "You look beautiful...Mrs. Rosenberg."

I giggled at the awkwardness with which he said my new name, but also savored the words. I was Hans' wife! I could not believe it.

The night passed with a flurry of dancing, men singing, and drinks being consumed at a surprisingly prodigious pace. Hans' friends were having quite the time harassing my friends and Ilse and Miriam were taking great pleasure in people watching. During that wonderful night, I danced with my mother, father, both cousins, my aunts, my uncles, and Liesl. Everyone I cared about in life was there and the room was filled with happiness. That's why Hans' news was so much harder to hear.

He pulled me aside right before midnight and brought me into the kitchen where it was much quieter. I thought he was going to kiss me again and my excitement began to build until he said, "Edith, you're not going to want to hear this, but it is important. The ship for Australia leaves in four days and we must be on it."

I could not believe my ears and almost screamed, "What? Hans, I thought we had weeks... months!"

"Edith, every day it gets harder to leave Austria. Our time is running out. This is our chance."

"But Hans, my mother and father and cousins!"

"You knew you were going to have to leave them at some point."

He was right. I knew, but I never expected it to be this soon. My heart had been so full moments earlier and now it ached with the pain of leaving my old life behind.

~

I stood by the door to our home. I had lived there since the day I was born. I had all my memories here. And now I was leaving it. I was giving up everything to escape. I was giving up everything to try and keep everything. Hans told me this was a life or death matter. The Rosenbergs were saving me. But still, I felt like I was losing my life by leaving. My heart felt like it was breaking into a million pieces. I would never know Vienna the same way again. I may never see my parents again. Goodbye home. Goodbye family. Goodbye.

Chapter 9:

Miriam

Vienna

Fall 1938

Edith was gone. She was probably on the ship to Australia by now. It was so strange to have a cousin and role model gone and gone so fast. I wondered if maybe I would leave soon. I missed

Edith and I hoped she was happy, but if I were to be entirely honest, other things distracted me.

Firstly, I had met a boy. I was playing in the street with Rachel and a few other girls in the neighborhood when I fell hard onto the dirt road. My knees and palms were scratched and bleeding so Rachel took me into the drug store to try and clean me up. While I limped in sniffling and pouting, I saw the most beautiful boy behind the counter. He looked older than me and was much taller. I tried to wipe away my snot and the dirt on me before he saw me, but Rachel had already drawn attention to us.

She had walked in with a, "Helloooo, you behind the counter! Can you help my friend here? She fell."

He responded in a strange accent, "Of course Ma'am. Let me grab some soap and water."

Rachel turned back and looked at me whispering, "Is he cute or is it just me?"

In a loud whisper I told her, "Obviously he is gorgeous. But how old is he?"

"Old." She said with dramatic sadness. "But, where did he come from? I've never seen him," she continued.

It turned out he was a family friend of the storeowner visiting from Poland and was 17 years old. He was trying to learn German and had a passion for the piano. Every day Rachel and I made up new reasons to visit the drug store. We had gone to pick up medicine for our sick neighbor, to check and see if there was a new hair product, and we had even tried fake falling in front of the store again. Today we were planning a new approach.

"Why don't we just ask him to come play with us and our friends?" Rachel suggested.

I laughed. "Of course we can't do that! He's older and young men his age don't 'play.'"

"But we can't just keep making up stupid excuses to visit that awful drug store. It's becoming obvious that we are stalking him," Rachel countered.

"Why don't we ask him to come to synagogue with us?" I gleefully suggested.

"I guess that isn't the worst idea you've ever had, Miriam."

With that we gleefully took off for the store.

"Hello Jakub!" Rachel coquettishly chimed as we walked in the store.

"Hello Rachel. How has your morning been?" He stammered in an awkward Polish accent. We found his accent to be charming, but admittedly, it sounded strange at times.

"Jakub, we were wondering if you would like to join us for services at the synagogue. I noticed you are never there and I thought you might enjoy it." I offered.

He coughed and looked around the room before saying, "Um girls I think you may have missed something. I'm catholic. I don't go to synagogue. I go to church."

Rachel and I exchanged confused looks as our faces turned tomato red. We had just assumed he was Jewish. Rachel apologized for our assumptions and we turned around and left quickly.

Once we were outside Rachel exclaimed, "How did we miss that?"

I, also shocked responded, "Rachel, he isn't Jewish! Do you know what that means? We can't love him!"

"Miriam, he's six years older than us. We were never going to marry him. Plus there are two of us. What were we going to do, share him?"

"Rachel, I don't care. All that stuff we can ignore. But a Catholic! I've never even met one let alone fallen in love with one!"

"You've met many Catholics before. But, you're right. Jews don't marry Gentiles. It is impossible. There's probably some commandment about that."

We went home after that slightly embarrassed and wondering whether it was morally ok to love a Catholic. When I got home and opened the door Mama asked what was wrong.

I mumbled, "I fell in love with a Catholic boy." She burst into a fit of laughter.

"Oh that Polish boy at the drug store! The whole neighborhood has been laughing at you and Rachel and your girlish attempts at flirting."

My face turned an even deeper shade of red as my mother laughed. I asked quietly, "Did everyone know he was Catholic?"

My mother laughed again and said, "Liebling, you wouldn't know this, but the adults know that no Jew is being let in from Poland right now. Plus I hadn't seen a yamaka on that boys head so I put two and two together." Noticing my embarrassment she added, "It's ok, Miriam. No one expected you to know that or to not flirt with him. He is an attractive young man."

With that she went back to the kitchen and I slumped over to my room.

~

A week later it was Yom Kippur and I had spent the morning in synagogue and the rest of the day peeling potatoes for breakfast. I was antsy, hungry, and bored. I had a year left until I had to fast, so I had been able to snack throughout the day. Papa and Mama had not, however, and they were intolerably grumpy. After services, Papa had gone into the Ringstrasse to visit Uncle Berthold and Mama and I had gone home.

Papa came home about an hour and a half later angry as can be. He slammed his fist on the table and sank into a chair. Mama rushed into the room asking what was wrong.

"I can't stand it, Berta." He responded curtly.

"Well, it's Yom Kippur, Joseph. Everyone's unhappy," Mama said.

"No Berta. This is different. Berthold and Regine are leaving Vienna. They are applying for visas out of the country."

"But how? Why? Everyone is making such a big deal out of nothing!"

"I can't explain, Berta, but they say they'll go anywhere. Berthold offered to get visas for us. What do you think?"

"I think I'll stay in my home. If they find somewhere good to go I'll consider it. But I will not go into a jungle or desert because of less than ideal political circumstances."

My parents had once again entered the endless debate. It was a debate over whether the Nazis mattered or not. It was about whether we should leave or not. It changed forms every day but there was always the same conversation. That is how the Nazis manifested in my life. They stayed out of our neighborhood for the most part so I never saw them and they never hurt me. But still, they were always discussed. If I didn't listen to Mama and Papa's conversations, I wouldn't even know they were here. I wasn't scared like Ilse or Edith. I was just bored of hearing about them.

Chapter 10:

Ilse

Vienna

Fall 1938

It was so strange how everything was
changing. Edith was gone, we went outside less,
and I was at a school just for Jews. My new school
was fine, but it was odd. I was learning things I had

learned three years ago and I was in the same class as George. I was also meeting the most curious people. One boy in my class wore all black with a long, white scarf and had little curls that popped out on the side of his head. He was extremely religious and serious, but I thought he looked rather funny and resembled a cartoon character.

I met a girl who had never been inside the Ringstrasse. I couldn't believe it. She lived less than five miles outside of the city, but she had never left her tiny neighborhood. There really was the most bizarre mix of people at this new school.

An even stranger thing about this school was that it was located far from home and George and I had to take the trolley together. It was scary taking the trolley with no parents and I did not like the neighborhood my new school was in. It was a rough part of town with smoke-clogged factories and beggars on the street. The only good thing about my school was Miriam would soon be in my class and I could not wait to have my cousin around to make the day a little more entertaining.

On Wednesday afternoon, George and I had just finished class and were walking outside when, to our surprise, we saw Mutti. We rushed towards her, excited by the surprise and relieved we didn't have to navigate the trolley alone.

"Mutti! Mutti! Mutti!" George cried.

"What are you doing here?" I asked her.

She responded, "We had a most exhausting customer and I needed a break from work so I thought I'd go see my two wonderful children."

After navigating the dirty streets of Vienna's outskirts and the grand boulevards of the Ringstrasse, we got back to the apartment having encountered no trouble. Mutti left right away to go back to the store and George and I were left alone.

A few months ago I would have spent that time doing my homework but now I found myself without anything to do. All my schoolwork was so simple I didn't have to bring any of it home. To make matters worse, none of my old neighborhood friends could play with me and I wasn't allowed to go outside.

Even the old nuisance of Helga was gone now. After the Nazis came, they banned gentiles from working for Jews and Helga had to leave us. While much of my childhood had been spent avoiding Helga's lectures and nags, it was like I had lost my second mother. Without Helga, George and I were alone and helpless.

Alone and bored, I walked around the house messing with my brother while he played with his toys. I jumped on my bed with no one there to scold me and then brushed my hair obsessively. I was bored out of my mind.

Two tedious hours later, Mutti and Papa were back in the apartment. They appeared out of sorts. Mutti's cheeks were bright red and she paced the apartment drumming her fingers against her collarbone. Papa seemed sort of depressed but I figured he was just tired as he was most days. He had a drink in the kitchen and then went to his room. Around 15 minutes after my parents came home, we began to hear strange noises coming from the street below. I heard a crash, like someone had just smashed a window. The crash was followed by shouting and then another crash until all the sounds were combined into one muddle of chaos. Mutti stopped straight in her tracks. Papa came rushing out of his room. George just whined about the noise. I was annoyed. How many times was this going to happen? We had already heard Hitler march in and now we were hearing whatever this mess was.

I was really boiling over with annoyance until I saw Mutti. In in my whole life I had almost never seen Mutti cry, but as I walked towards the window I saw a tear trickle down her cheek. Papa put his arm around her and I noticed how much older Papa and Mutti looked. Mutti then turned towards us, frantically wiped away her tears and began to say, "George, Ilse. Your Papa and I lost our store today.'

Four million different thoughts went through my head but before I could vocalize any of them, Mutti continued.

"The Nazis have taken all businesses and jobs from any known Jews. A young officer walked in this evening and said 'leave now.' He didn't lay a hand on us, but we lost the store."

My jaw dropped. That corner shop had been in my life since I was born. Before I was in school I had spent countless hours sitting on the counter and watching customers. Some of my most exciting days had been spent there. I once met Hedy Lamarr there when she was filming a movie in Vienna. She came into our store and purchased a snakeskin notebook. It was exhilarating. Another time a magician came in and showed me card tricks for almost an hour. That store was our lifeline and it was gone.

Papa sighed and then continued with the next bit of news, "No one is sure what's happening, but from what we saw it looks as if there is some sort of riot going on."

Mutti embraced us and Papa walked up wrapping his arms around our whole family. We were a combination of sweat, tears, fear, anger, and sadness.

Mutti softly offered, "Why don't I make dinner?"

Papa solemnly nodded, dropped his arms, and turned on the radio while pulling George into his lap. Together the five of us sat listening to the radio and hearing the noises outside. I never went to look out the window. I was too scared. Instead we sat. Our dinner got cold as none of us were hungry. We later learned from the radio that the riot was a pogrom against Jews. Synagogues, Jewish neighborhoods, and businesses were targeted. I went to bed around 1 AM as no one had the energy to get up and put George and me to bed. I didn't sleep that night. The noise continued until the early morning. I cried and I buried myself under the sheets. Nothing was right anymore.

The next morning I walked into the dining room and saw Mutti and Papa in their clothes from the night before. Mutti's eyes were red and Papa's hair was standing straight up. They looked horrible.

"Hello darlings. How did you sleep last night??" Mutti asked quietly.

"I didn't," I responded. George said the same.

"Well children, I'm sorry you had to witness a night like last night, and I'm sorry you didn't sleep, but we have something very important to tell you."

George and I leaned in. George was excited to hear the news but I was wary as nothing good could be announced after a night like that.

Papa continued, "Your mother and I have decided that our family will be leaving Austria."

I was stunned. Then I was a little excited. I
would be leaving everything I'd ever known, but I'd
get to see Edith again in Australia, or so I assumed
until Papa continued.

"We have visas to travel to Trinidad. It is a
British territory and it's a tropical island so it will
be an adventure!" He tried very hard to sound
positive.

"Also," Mutti added, "Your father will not
be leaving the apartment until we leave for Trinidad
in December. We heard that Jewish men are being
pulled of the streets and sent to prison. Ilse and
George, you aren't going to school today as we
should all stay inside today."

George protested as he evidently had no idea
what was going on. He said he needed to see his
friends at school. I stayed quiet. I wasn't going to
see Edith and I was traveling across the world to a
completely foreign place.

Mutti interrupted my thoughts by asking,
"Ilse, are you fine with this?"

I gave a simple nod and approving grunt. I
didn't matter what I thought. We were leaving
because we needed to.

After that conversation the rest of the day went by in a haze. Our building was mainly Jewish so neighbors flooded in and out of our apartment sharing news and stories. Our beautiful synagogue was reported to be the only synagogue that wasn't burned, but it had been ransacked and defaced. The Nazis had also taken a list of congregation members, which included us. Outside, the streets were a mess of broken glass and all the stores were shut down. The rioters had been men and women from all over town with ages as young as seven. Franz and Rolf Schroeder, my former classmates, had apparently thrown bricks into our store window.

Of course, I never saw any of this myself. I couldn't confirm that it was true. But trapped in my apartment, our neighbors' news became my reality day in and day out. Later, as we finally left the apartment and tried to resume our lives, I would witness the devastation for myself.

Chapter 11:

Edith

The Ocean

Fall 1938

God, I missed home. I missed dry land and a
stable ground. Everything about life on a boat was
chaotic. The boat was constantly rocking with water
splashing up onto the deck. I could barely sleep at
night because the boat was heaving so forcefully.
The food was also particularly foul. Each meal,
there was either soup or cold chicken served with a
side of green beans and a roll of soggy bread. It was

a far cry from the decadent desserts at Demel's. Rats also ran all through steerage, huddling closest to little puddles of water. Fortunately we were staying in second class so we didn't have to deal with these rats at night.

Life on the boat had a few consolations. I liked seeing the ocean every day and being able to wake up and smell salt water and fresh sea air. I also liked the people on the boat and was learning so many new things through my new acquaintances. One passenger was a large, confident Irish woman who spoke with a heavy accent and was constantly yelling at the staff. She had three children, all with matching fiery red hair. Her children were the hardest working kids I had ever met as this woman didn't tolerate idleness. She had left her husband in Ireland and decided to start a new life in Australia of all places. We soon became friends and I would come to her room and help her sew and knit clothes for her children. While we worked, she gave me advice on marriage, cooking, and plenty of other things. She would say, "Listen child, I didn't have a good marriage, obviously. My husband and I stopped loving each other the moment we got married. But because I was so bad at marriage, I can give you some good advice. Never care too much about what your husband does in his free time. The second you start to nag him, he stops caring about you, and everything falls apart. Being married is about behaving at home, not everywhere."

She also would also say, "Always burn dinner. If you burn dinner every day, you can make your kids and your husband indebted to you when you don't burn dinner. If you always make good food, they'll never be grateful."

The woman was crazy, but I liked her.

I also met a strange British scientist on the boat. He had been a professor in England until he got bored of the classroom and start researching plants in Australia. He showed me drawings of the many exotic plant and animal species that lived in Australia. I learned all about these things called kangaroos. They had a little pocket to carry their babies in and they jumped around on two feet. I found them hilarious as they reminded me of characters I used to make up in my head when I was little.

The boat had also introduced me to the wonders of adult life. In Vienna I was always a young girl on her way to womanhood. Here, I was a woman, a young wife of a future lawyer. I was invited to the parties that were hosted after dinner. Sometimes Hans and I were invited to first class parties where I had to borrow a gown and gloves from another young wife in first class. At these soirees, we danced formally and socialized with wealthy families from Australia and England.

At other times we were invited to steerage parties where we wore our day clothes and danced to loud, fast-paced music. At these parties, there were leftovers from dinner and barrels of beer. The men and women danced and laughed together and, every once in a while, there would be a brawl between two men. It was here that I had my first sip of an alcoholic beverage. I was unimpressed; beer tasted like dirty water. Hans loved it and drank till he was full almost every night. On some nights I would leave him and go to bed early. Shortly after this became our routine I began to notice Hans taking interest in a particularly attractive young woman. She had beautiful blonde hair (unlike my dull brunette coloring) and she had the smallest waist on the boat. She was not high class and the men on the boat viewed her as a prize they could easily win. I detested her. She put me on the defensive and made me start questioning the shape of my lips or thinness of my wrists, things I had never thought of before.

I took my Irish friend's words seriously and tried not to care about Hans' interest in this woman. Instead, I focused on developing my relationship with Hans. I tried to take tea with him every afternoon and learn about him a little more each day. He loved the ocean and constantly talked about wanting to swim. He also, to my displeasure, enjoyed smoking far too much. Whenever his parents weren't around, he had a cigarette between his lips. Hans and I couldn't be typical newlyweds yet because we were on a crowded boat with his parents, but I often thought about our future life together in Australia. Would we live alone? Share a house with his parents? And then there was the idea of children. That scared me for multiple reasons. Firstly, I couldn't imagine carrying my own baby in my body and then having to suffer through hours of painful labor. Secondly, I was going to have the life of a baby in my hands and it was going to be entirely my job to make sure my babies grew up into good people. I was barely done being raised myself; that was just too much responsibility.

My most recent adventure involved learning the English language. Hans' mother had learned English in school when she was planning on studying in England, so she took it upon herself to teach me English. Hans already knew some from his mother, so most lessons were just she and I. Today we were going over vocabulary terms.

"So Edith, l-e-a-d means both to guide someone and the material pencils are made of. When it means to guide, it is pronounced with a long 'e' and when it refers to the material in pencils, it is pronounced with a short 'e'. When the verb form is put into the past tense, the spelling changes to 'l-e-d' and it is pronounced with a short 'e', like the pencil," she explained in a manner that made it sound like it should be simple.

I, clearly not a fast learner, simply replied, "What."

"I know it is confusing, Edith, but the language will only get easier as you hear people speaking it. You can already make simple conversation with some of the British folk on the boat. Pretty soon it'll be a breeze for you."

While I hoped she was right and I would soon be on my way to understanding English, I had little faith in my abilities. I had learned French and a little Dutch with ease when I was young. Languages were typically not difficult for me, but English proved more difficult than almost anything I had ever done.

The chaotic and challenging life on the boat made me long for my parents' company and I hoped I would see them soon. I was so scared for the difficulties of my new life and I knew Mutter's way with words would have helped me. The language, children, Hans, and being a grown woman all seemed like too much for me. I had never been a particularly religious person like Ilse and Miriam, but I began praying every night for my family's safety. I prayed mainly for my parents, but also for my poor little cousins and my aunts and uncles. I couldn't receive letters on the boat, but I hoped when we docked I would hear news of their safety and maybe even of their leaving and coming to Australia. I knew it was a far-fetched dream, but I still had hope.

After the English lesson, Hans' mother and I both went off to bed, I exhausted by the lesson and her seasick. I went to bed feeling heartbroken. I missed my old life. I missed being a young girl. I missed dry land. I missed good brisket. I missed my father. But, above all, I missed my mother. 17 was simply too young for me to be taken away from her.

Chapter 12

Miriam

Vienna

Fall 1938

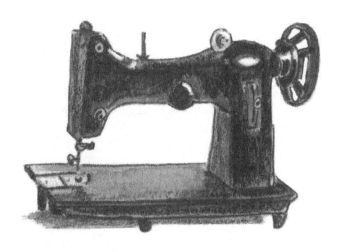

Our streets are littered with trash and broken glass. While we were used to gravel streets and occasional litter on the sides of the road, this was unlike anything I had seen before. Ever since that one horrific night, shops have been in disrepair and our entire neighborhood looks like a war scene. The synagogue was burned down to the ground with pieces of its precious Torah blowing across the streets. When Mama first saw the synagogue she began to weep uncontrollably. She started frantically gathering fragments of parchment desperately hoping she could put the Torah back together. The sight halfway frightened and halfway embarrassed me and I eventually resorted to turning away and trying to ignore her.

Late into the night people had taken to the streets burning buildings and breaking glass of Jewish homes and shops. Our neighborhood was hit the worst because there are so many Jews here. I had never cried harder than that night.

In the week that has past, local families have been trying to clean up the mess. Some do it in the manic, half-mad way my mother did. Others calmly and quickly pick up trash, wiping away the occasional tears. We mainly see women and children. Men are almost never on the streets anymore. After that night, the Nazis started randomly taking Jewish men to prison, so any with sense stayed inside. To my mother's great pain, my father was refusing to lock himself up. He walked the streets freely acting as if nothing had happened. He stopped trying to hide things from me and spoke frankly about his opinions on the Nazis. He had lost all care and Mama had lost all sense.

The pogrom had also affected the neighborhood where my father's store was, so we no longer had a store or an income. There was no way he could get a job with all the prison roundups, so Mama and I tried to find work. We applied to work at grocery stores, pharmacies, and dress shops. We eventually found work at a linen factory. All the owners cared about was that the workers met their quota not whether we were Jewish. Mama and I started work today.

I walked into the kitchen dressed in our factory-issued uniform. It was a rough gray dress that scratched at my skin and ended at my low calf. The dress was made for older, taller women and hung off my body like a sack. I slipped on my winter boots and wrapped myself in a ragged shawl as it was getting increasingly cold outside.

Mama trudged into the kitchen with heavy bags under her eyes. She yawned, scratched her head and then said, "We have to be there in 30 minutes and it's a 20 minute walk. Eat something quick."

There was no emotion or nuance in her voice anymore. She had been fighting with Papa, our new job was wearing her out, and she seemed frightened about what might befall us. With Edith gone and Ilse's family leaving, my mother felt we were making a grave mistake. She worried that we were all going to be sent to prison or killed. Every time she saw a soldier on the street she flinched and cowered. Only a month ago, my mother had been confident and unafraid. Of course, everything changed after Kristallnacht.

I grabbed four hard boiled eggs for us to split and glanced at our empty pantry. We were becoming poorer and poorer every day.

"Mama," I whispered, trying not to wake Papa up. "Let's go."

She gave a nod and started moving towards the door.

We walked in silence for the next 20 minutes with only an occasional grunt or sigh. Once we got near the factory I began to hear a growing murmur of voices. As we reached the factory, the murmur turned into a clamor I was amazed by the number of workers milling around in front of the factory door. Girls were chatting with each other and tying each others bonnets while sharing lukewarm coffee. Mama was the oldest there and I was the youngest. We didn't fit in.

One of the older girls in the crowd spotted us and walked up saying, "You two must be our newest workers."

Mama stared blankly as though she hadn't heard anyone speak, so I answered, "Yes, this is our first day. Where should we go?"

The woman laughed a little to herself and responded, "You're so naive!" She pinched my cheek. "When the bell rings go up one level and to the left. You'll find our sewing machines with beginner work. Good luck!"

She was far too happy for five in the morning. I was so tired and every time I yawned, I felt like I was going to faint. I was an 11 year old girl with an unresponsive mother in a gigantic factory and I was scared. I had only worked a sewing machine once and I didn't know who to ask for help.

A giant bell sounded from the building and a wave of young women flowed towards the gigantic doors. I grabbed Mama's hands and tried to pull her along with the tide. I walked up the stairs and went to the left just like the woman had told me. I was met with a wall of office doors.

I was in the wrong place. Panicking, I raced to the other side of the stairs dragging my mother behind me. There were no sewing machines there either. I tried to figure out where the other women were headed...and I was stuck in the middle of an unfamiliar building with tears streaming down my face. All of the sudden I began to hear a growing noise. The floor started to shake. The racket sounded like a frantic hive of bees. I heard it coming from above me. That's when I realized that noise was the humming of sewing machines. I gave a little cheer and ran upstairs. At the left there was a woman surveying younger workers. I figured that must be the beginner area. I walked over, grateful to finally be in the right place. The woman in charge swiveled her head around and gave me a piercing and disapproving stare. She screeched, "Are you our two missing girls? Why are you late? The bell rang ten minutes ago. And why are you so old and you so young? Stations 15 and 16. Now!"

I scrambled to get to my station and was prepared to start my work until I looked at the machine and realized I had no materials and didn't know how to work the machine.

The Screecher threw a piece of white cloth and me and said, "Make a straight hem."

I knew what a hem was so I thought I could work my way through this. I fumbled with my machine until I found a switch. Miraculously, the machine was already threaded so I folded over the edge of the sheet, put my foot on the pedal, and prayed the needle wouldn't go through my finger.

The needle never hit my finger and after one day I had successfully hemmed six full sheets. They weren't pretty, but they were done. I was even more exhausted than in the morning and trudged home, mother in tow, only to crash on my bed. I fell asleep as soon as my body hit the sheets.

~

I woke up in the middle of the night in a hot sweat. I heard crashing and a scream. I thought it was a dream until I felt the sweat on my body and realized I was awake. I got out of bed and walked to the window. Across the street, two soldiers were dumping papers and belongings out of a second story window while another held back a crying woman. A fourth grabbed a man I assumed to be her husband and shoved him into a car. The woman was shrieking and crying while the man reached out for her only to drop his hands when the soldier knocked him back in the car. I quickly closed the drapes. I stood there, heart thumping hard against my rib cage. Hot tears poured down my face and I hoped Rachel was ok. She only lived one house down from that family. I longed for us to leave with Ilse's family. My knees buckled, so I curled up on the floor right there until 5 AM the next morning.

Chapter 13:

Ilse

Holland

Winter 1938

Tonight we leave for Trinidad. I haven't stopped crying since I woke up this morning. I spent the last week saying my goodbyes, but to be entirely honest, I didn't have a lot of people to say goodbye to as most of my friends had stopped talking to me months ago and Helga had been forced to leave our family already. It was the little people that I never thought would be important that I had to say bye to. I said bye to Mr. Wilensky at his grocery store and Ms. Kaltenbach at the dress shop. I said a fond goodbye to my favorite cake at Demel's and cried when I saw the ice rink for the last time.

The hardest part though was saying bye to my family, especially Miriam. She was my dearest cousin and my best friend. I hadn't known a day in my life where she wasn't at most 15 kilometers away. Yesterday, I went to her house to say my final goodbye. It had been a month since Kristallnacht, but glass, trash, and paper still littered the streets. Mutti, Papa, and George walked next to me solemnly. Papa knocked.

Uncle Joseph cracked the door open and quietly said, "come in, come in."

His face was dirty and wrinkled. The light in Aunt Berta's eyes had dimmed and her mouth remained thin and flat. Her shoulders were hunched over and her skin hung loosely off her face. I barely recognized her. Miriam was still cheerful and she ran towards me letting out a big, "Illllssseee!!" But, she too looked tired and different.

She threw her arms around me and hugged me tight while I wheezed, "Miriam, you're going to kill me."

She responded with a laugh and said, "I'm just going to miss you so much. I don't want to let you go."

"Me too but...I have to leave."

"I know." Her eyes were begging to come with me and I just wanted to tell her that we would always be together. But, of course I couldn't. Her parents had already refused, despite my constant begging.

Miriam started to cry. She clutched my arm like a small child and let the tears flow. We stood there for a minute until Mutti tapped me.

"We have to leave, Ilse. Say goodbye," Mutti told me.

Miriam squeezed me and I turned to leave. As Uncle Joseph closed the door, I turned and caught a glance of my cousin. I prayed it wouldn't be the last time.

Today, I was still recovering from saying goodbye to Miriam. I had a lot of work to do though. I had to choose my favorite things to pack. We had only one trunk to pack everything we would need in and we weren't allowed to bring any money. A couple of days ago Mutti, unbeknownst to Papa, went down to our store and in the prettiest, sweetest voice asked the Nazi stationed there if she could quickly grab a trunk to pack our stuff in. He fortunately let her take the trunk and while he walked to the front of the store, she quickly stuffed everything of value that she could into the trunk. The problem then was that Mutti couldn't carry it by herself. So, the Nazi helped her carry it up to our apartment. When Papa opened the door to our apartment and saw a Nazi, he almost screamed in horror. Miraculously, this particular Nazi was rather stupid and never asked why the trunk was so heavy. I learned all this while Mutti and Papa screamed at each other about how Mutti almost got us all killed.

Eventually, they got around to telling George and me that we had to pack two outfits, our most prized possessions, and one pair of shoes. Mutti and Papa were packing the rest of the trunk with things we absolutely needed or could sell. I chose to bring a loose skirt, white blouse, brown oxfords, and my autograph book which was filled with notes from my favorite people. It wasn't much, but it would do.

I looked into my closet at that beautiful velvet ice skating dress. The one I wore on that day back in February which had been so peaceful and simple. I never would have guessed my life would change this much in 10 months. I was going to miss that dress and I worried that I would never get to ice skate again. Trinidad was supposed to be tropical and warm year round.

~

After hours of helping Mutti sort through our belongings and trying our hardest to pack everything in tight, we were finally ready to leave. Our train for Amsterdam, where we would get on the boat, was an overnight ride. Papa and Mutti heaved the trunk into the elevator and George and I followed close behind. Before Papa closed the door, we all took one last look at the apartment. The apartment looked as it always had. The paintings still hung straight, the furniture was all still there with Mutti's decorative pillows placed and fluffed perfectly. I wondered if the neighbors would even notice we were gone.

But more than anything, I couldn't believe we were really leaving. This was my last glance at my home. I spent hours on that living room floor and almost every meal at that dining room table. It was the strangest feeling to leave this home.

And then Papa closed the door. With that, we all scooted into the elevator and went down to street level. It was almost nightfall so most people were settling in for dinner. We walked through the nearly empty street dragging our huge trunk until we reached the street car.

I watched my home city swish by as the street car sped through our neighborhood. I saw my old school and the Hofburg palace and the market being packed up for the day. I watched fashionable young women pass by poor beggars and the local drunks. And as we got closer to the government buildings, I started to see soldiers marching in lines with shiny boots and stiff uniforms. I was reminded then that my city was no longer really mine. We were leaving for a reason.

The streetcar reached the end of its track at the train station and we got off. Our train was sitting there waiting for us and without even looking back (I had done that far too many times this week) I got on the train and sat down. Mutti laid her scarf over me as an ersatz blanket and I fell asleep before the train had even left the station.

~

When I woke up, we were in Holland. My throat felt sore and I rubbed the sleep out of my eyes. There was frost on the window and Mutti was rubbing her hands together and blowing hot breath on them. I groggily asked to no one in particular, "Where are we?"

Papa responded, "We're thirty minutes from Amsterdam."

George was still asleep across from me and Mutti and Papa didn't seem to be in a talking mood so I pressed my nose up against the window and looked out at Holland. I had never been there before but I had heard wondrous stories of Amsterdam from girls at my school. From the train though I just saw an idyllic countryside with rows and rows of tulips.

When the train pulled up to the station there was a rush of people. It was the morning work rush and people swarmed the station. Papa and Mutti once again awkwardly lugged the trunk through the crowds with Mutti pausing occasionally to catch her breath. I held George's hand and tried not to run into people. I watched as men, still drunk from the night before, slumped against the walls and as we approached the docks I watched fishermen and dock workers smoke cigarettes and spit into the water. They smelled like old fish and were covered in rubber gear. It wasn't a pleasant sight.

Mutti and Papa found a bench near the dock to sit and gather ourselves at. The four of us sat down together and George, who had not said a word since we left our apartment, abruptly said, "I didn't know we had an ocean."

Our parents hadn't heard him, engrossed in figuring out our tickets for the boat, but I responded, "George, do you seriously think we are still in Vienna? We're in Amsterdam, stupid." I guess not everything had changed.

Chapter 14:
Edith

Australia

Winter 1939

Well, we made it to dry land. This morning we finally docked in Sydney Harbor. I was so excited to get off the boat and feel solid ground that I didn't even catch a glimpse of the grand city in front of me. As soon as I felt the boat stop moving, I grabbed my purse and Hans' hand and took off for the exit. The one problem was that Hans got held back in the crowd somehow so I had to take off on my own. I was seconds away from throwing up. I ran down the ramp and practically collapsed when my feet hit the dock. Thank God! I was so tired of that boat!

In the midst of my celebration I saw Hans walk off the boat with a red face and a woman grabbing at his coat. It was her. That blonde girl Hans had been fooling around with on the boat was clinging to him like he was hers. The nerve of that woman! I didn't mind a brief fling but to follow him off the boat was something else all together. At least Hans seemed to be rejecting her. As I watched their interaction, the woman's voice started to get louder.

She practically screamed, "You love me! I know you do! We were supposed to get off the boat together and get married!"

Hans retorted, "I am married, Susana!"

"But you love me!"

"No I don't. We're back on land now, back to real life."

The woman started wailing and tugging as he pulled away. Everyone was staring by now and Hans' mother came storming towards him. I've seen a lot of angry Jewish mothers in my 17 years but I had never seen anyone like this. She grabbed her son by the arm and dragged him away from his collapsing blonde.

She yelled, "Hans you have been married 1 month and you already had an affair? This is not how I raised you. Where is your poor wife? Oy vey, what a disappointment!"

Hans sheepishly looked around only to make eye contact with me. He quickly looked down at his feet and awkwardly kicked at a pebble while his face turned scarlet.

I was calm and poised. Yes, I was embarrassed but I was stronger than that. I was going to start my new life and forget all of this. It didn't matter; Hans had rejected the girl anyways. I smiled back at Hans and his mother and walked towards the taxi stand.

Hans followed me and tried to get me to stop, "I'm so sorry Edith, so so sorry. It meant nothing. I wasn't used to being married and I promise it'll never happen again."

I matter-of-factly responded, "Hans, I understand. I'm not mad. Let's just find where we're staying."

While I understood what he did, it still hurt. But all I could think about was getting some sleep. I had felt exhausted and irritable for most of the boat trip. I was out of sorts.

Hans' father got us a cab and we all piled in. Our things were being shipped from the ship to a house Hans' parents had purchased ahead of time. Luckily, they had arranged everything before the Nazis had closed their bank account.

As I sat in the tiny cab, I finally got a good look at our new country. The sky was such a pure blue and faded seamlessly into the water. The flowers were orange and green and red and the buildings were the brightest of whites. It was December and yet the sun shone brilliantly in the sky. It was a pleasant change from the grey skies of Vienna. I only wished my parents were here to enjoy this with me. I was hoping we'd hear something from them as soon as we reached the house.

As we passed through Sydney, I noticed the strange mix of people. I rolled down the window and heard a mix of languages and accents and noticed all different colors of people. In Vienna, everyone was the same shade of pasty white. Here I saw a bronzed woman arm in arm with an equally tanned man who bid hello to an African looking man while an Asian man walked around them. It was fascinating.

~

We pulled into the driveway of our new house in Melbourne. It was medium sized with nice garden in front. The house had almost 100 feet on either side of it and had space in the front and back. I had never seen a house with this much outdoor space. There was only one story, no elevator or winding staircase. It felt like a cottage.

I walked in and went straight to the smaller of the bedrooms. I threw my bag on a chair and fell asleep immediately. I don't know why I kept falling asleep.

When I woke up I had an inescapable urge to vomit. I ran to the adjacent bathroom and threw up liquid as I really had not eaten today. I felt horrible. And then I knew why.

"Hans," I whispered quietly as I walked out of the bathroom.

"What, Edith?" he responded.

"I think... I think I might be pregnant."

He stared back completely shocked by my news and said, "That is wonderful, I think."

Small tears started gathering in the corner of my eyes. He didn't sound pleased and I didn't want a baby yet. I left the room to go check for a note from my parents. There was nothing: no message or signal or communication whatsoever. I was so alone. Hours ago I had been enjoying the sun and everything about this place and now I felt just as depressed as I had felt on the boat. I didn't know how this marriage was going to work for the rest of my life if it couldn't even work for a month. I didn't want children with Hans. I didn't want to bring a child into this world. I couldn't have a baby until I saw my own mother again.

But the truth was that I didn't have a choice. I was pregnant. I was going to have a baby and unless my mother could get here in nine months, I would have it alone. There was nothing I could do to fix this. I had no options. I was going to bring a baby into my miserable world with my underwhelming husband and without my mother.

Chapter 15:

Miriam

Vienna

Spring 1939

It's been months since Ilse left and my life is unrecognizable. There were too many round ups in my neighborhood, so we left our house and moved in with my Aunt Charlotte and Uncle Hugo. Since Edith left, they have been lonely and my parents thought our family needed to be together to brace the difficult year ahead. I did enjoy having everyone near and living in a nicer neighborhood, but life was still miserable. No one had a job anymore, and all Jewish bank accounts had been taken away, so we had no money. Mama occasionally knitted scarves and hats to sell to the few neighbors who pitied us and didn't hate Jews.

I never left the apartment. Ever. We weren't necessarily in hiding, but we tried to keep our presence as hidden as possible. My mother and Aunt Charlotte switched off leaving the apartment to get food and tried to leave early in the morning or late at night to avoid seeing soldiers. Most all Jewish shops were closed, so my aunt and Mama had to travel to a different neighborhood to buy our basic food with the small funds we had left.

Papa and Uncle Hugo never left the building as they were scared of being taken in a round-up and I was just scared of whatever else lay outside. Our apartment had run out of electricity because we could no longer pay the bills. Luckily, we still had running water.

Life was bearable, but I was miserable. On the nights we didn't have dinner I was starving and grumpy. On the nights we did, I was a little more full, but still grumpy. I missed fresh air and my old life. I was cold without heat in the apartment and my one release was looking out the window at the street below. I would watch the people below talk with each other and go about their day as I imagined what they were saying or doing. I imagined the man in the big fur coat was bringing candy home to his grandchildren and the woman in the large hat was his much younger, beautiful wife who married him because he could afford things like fur coats.

I also missed my cousins tremendously. Every day since Ilse had been gone I had become more and more lonely. I hoped she was safely on the boat and we all prayed Edith was happy in Australia with Hans. I had never really gotten to know Uncle Hugo and Aunt Charlotte, but the countless hours spent together made me like them more. They had put aside a small amount of money to send Edith letters and tried as often as possible to reach her. I felt sad for them watching their daughter leave. They kept a small photo of her by their bed and my aunt mentioned her in every conversation, always giving the same sad smile.

I couldn't imagine what my parents would do without me. Mama had gotten better since we moved because she had Aunt Charlotte's company, but she still seemed empty and lacked energy to do basic chores. Papa was quiet and spent most of his days sitting next to Uncle Hugo with a week-old copy of the paper scrutinizing every word. I had always known my parents loved me, but these days it seemed like I was the one thing keeping them sane. The only time I see them smile is when I dance for everyone at night or draw an exaggerated portrait of my Uncle Hugo's mustache and double chin.

While I hated my boring life, a small part of me knew I was still lucky. Papa and Uncle Hugo weren't in prison and none of us had been subjected to horrible humiliation or harm like other Jews in the neighborhood had. Looking out the window at the street was my favorite pastime, but it also let me see things I wish hadn't. One day, as I sat by the window, I noticed a Nazi officer. Whenever a Nazi walked down the street, I ducked away from the window. But this time I saw him grab a woman by her hair before I could hide. Once I saw that I couldn't look away. I watched as he grabbed her and threw her down on the street. She crawled away from him in a panic and looked up desperately at the people walking by her. The soldier began barking orders. Typically I imagine what people on the street are saying, but this time I did everything in my power to avoid thinking about it.

As the soldier berated the woman, a truck pulled up and several more people got out. They all fell to their knees near a piece of graffiti on the street and began scrubbing. The soldier kicked the woman and she joined the rest of the scrubbers. A few people seemed to let out screams of pain and I wondered why they were doing that. No one was hurting them. I didn't understand why scrubbing was so painful.

As I stared down confused, Mama came up to me. She cuddled up to me and said, "What is so fascinating about the street today?"

I didn't answer. She looked down, let out a little whimper, and pulled me back. I asked, "Why are they in pain. I don't understand."

She stoically replied, "I don't think those buckets are full of water."

"What are they full of then?"

"Acid."

She kept her arms around me for another second or two and then, without another word, got up and went to her room. I looked down at the street once more, closed the curtains, and followed her.

Since that day at the window, I experienced the true feeling of pure fear. Since the Nazis came and everything had happened I had either been annoyed, sad, lonely, or worried but I had never been truly terrified. Even during Kristallnacht or when I heard about the round-ups I wasn't scared for myself. I had never witnessed actual violence. But, after seeing that woman in the street, I began to see everything in a darker shade. The shouts that had just been neighborhood noises became screams and the creaks in the floorboards at night sent goose bumps down my back.

As I lay in bed I began to hear loud stomping noises. I thought for a moment that my new hypersensitivity might be tricking me until Mama woke up.

She sat up and whispered, "Did you hear that?"

"Yes." I quickly whispered back.

Then Papa woke up right as Aunt Charlotte and Uncle Hugo ran into our room.

Uncle Hugo was the first to speak, "That sound… It sounds like Nazi boots. Everyone be quiet."

We all huddled together and listened to the evenly spaced stomps get closer. The stomps stopped and there was a knock. We all thought the same thing: is that our door? No one knew what to do. So we waited in silence.

Our prayers were answered when we heard a door down the hall open. A woman spoke in rushed French and a man whispered back in German. The conversation then switched to English. What kinds of people use three different languages in one conversation? And what kind of Nazi street thug knows three different languages?

There were three more boot stomps and then the door slammed shut. We didn't hear any boots walk back down the stairs, but we all stayed still until we were sure the coast was clear. Aunt Charlotte was the first to move a let out a huge sigh, "He must not have been a Nazi. Thank God!"

"Ok, back to bed," Uncle Hugo said with a yawn.

The adults acted like it wasn't a big deal because it was a false alarm, but I couldn't let go that fast. As I climbed back into bed I thought of those boot steps and that soldier on the street. I thought about how we were living in the midst of a nightmare. We were one soldier away from prison or death or worse. I had never been so scared in my life.

Chapter 16:

Ilse

Trinidad

Spring 1941

I'm fifteen today! That is basically
adulthood. When Edith turned fifteen she was
allowed to go places on her own and she got an
allowance. Oh, Vienna! And Edith! And money for
an allowance! It's been two years since I left

Vienna and almost three since I said goodbye to Edith. I haven't heard anything from her or Miriam since I left. Even if they tried to reach me, I doubt a letter would get through as almost my entire time in Trinidad has been spent cooped up in this camp, cut off from the rest of the world. Because we came from German-controlled Austria, when Britain declared war on Germany we were brought to this camp. Back in 1939 when we heard about the war we almost cried tears of joy. Mutti explained that this could put an end to Hitler and could save our relatives. It was the best news about our family we could've heard. But of course, I've learned that nothing is ever completely bad or completely good. A group of handsome British soldiers showed up at our door a week later and told us to pack.

We were supposedly a high risk family because my parents worked in a hotel bar in Port of Spain. The soldiers claimed that we could easily be spies collecting information from travelers who passed through the hotel. Mutti repeatedly told them that we were Jews fleeing Austria and had absolutely no interest in helping the Germans but the soldiers simply dismissed her.

We reported to a boat which then took us to a small island where we were to live until the camp on the mainland was built. Days there were fairly boring as there wasn't anywhere to go or anything to do. Fortunately, we were only there for a couple months.

The main camp, where we live now, isn't horrible; it isn't great either. We make do with what we have. Most of the other people here are refugees (that's what they call us) and almost everyone speaks German. After weeks of enduring the bland British diet, we asked the kitchen staff to let us cook German and Austrian food. Someone should really tell England that Germans and Austrians make far better sausage. Some days we don't get food because of the food shortage on the island the fact that we are technically prisoners didn't really put us on the top of the ration list. Those days tend to be worse than others.

The children don't work in the camp so I spend most of my days in a muggy and dark schoolroom. They couldn't afford to bring teachers to the camp so everyday I get on a bus and a camp guard takes us to the nearby school. We mainly study English and the history of England and Trinidad but every once in a while we do science projects or learn math equations.

Today was my birthday, but I still had to go to school. I woke up to George's feet in my face and the musty smell of sweat. We all shared one room with two cots and in May the heat was just starting to get unbearable. I pushed his feet to the side and rolled onto the ground. I had been effectively sleeping on the floor for two years now. I grabbed my uniform and tired to change as fast as possible while hoping nobody would wake up and see me. Three years ago I wouldn't have cared but back then I looked like a little boy. Now I'm fifteen. Can you believe that? I have long hair and I'm five foot five inches. I look like a young woman, finally. Once I got my uniform and shoes on, I grabbed my autograph book. I had gotten it for my twelfth birthday in Vienna and I always made sure to have a page reserved for my birthday. Just as I was tucking my book away again, Mutti woke up and rolled over.

She yawned while saying, "Happy Birthday, liebling. Ich liebe dich."

"I love you too, Mutti." I was trying to use more English, but I could never stop calling my mother Mutti.

"Do you have your work done for school today?" She asked me.

"Yes. I did it all last night."

"Well, you're up awfully early then. Are you going to see Hans?"

"Yes, hopefully."

Hans is my new boyfriend. I met him at school and learned he was also in the camp. We weren't in the same class as me but we saw each other every so often on the school yard and around the camp. He was my first real boyfriend and (of course!) he had the same name as Edith's husband. Edith and I were both romantically involved with a Hans.

My Hans was cute with dimples, blue eyes, and a puff of blonde hair. He made me laugh and was nice enough. I liked him and I really liked having a boyfriend. All the other girls in the camp were jealous, especially because I got the only blonde boy.

In a normal situation, my parents would never know about Hans and might have disapproved, but in the camp I couldn't hide anything and they were grateful I had some distraction. Hans and I couldn't go on dates outside of camp but sometimes he would take me out to the fruit orchards or to a soccer game between the kitchen staff and the orchard staff.

As I finished putting my book away, I said goodbye to Mutti and walked outside to go find Hans. He must've gotten up earlier than me because when I walked out, he was walking right towards me with his hands behind his back. When we reached each other I looked around and then gave him a quick peck on the cheek.

He turned a bright shade of red and said, "Happy Birthday, Ilse! I have this for you."

He thrust his hands forward and revealed a roll of bread and small bouquet of flowers and weeds. I don't think he knew the difference between a daisy and a dandelion but it was very sweet. I devoured the roll and thanked him sheepishly.

"We have thirty minutes before breakfast starts. Do you want to see the sunrise at the orchard?" I asked.

"Of course but let's get to breakfast a few minutes early so we can get first pick." He responded, focused solely on getting a good meal.

We walked to the field as the sky started to lighten up. We watched as the sky went from dark blue to orange to pink to yellow to light blue. I didn't like to reflect on the past too much, but my birthday sunrise made me think back on the time that had passed since Hitler came and my old life ended. It had been a tough couple of years, but I could feel things getting better. I had a feeling that the war would be over soon and that I would see all my cousins and aunts and uncles and Helga. I would bring Hans with me back to Vienna and he even could meet the other Hans. This future was so close I could almost feel it. Of course, there was no way I could know if the war was ending anytime soon. I hadn't seen a newspaper or message since arriving in the camp. They put in this camp because they thought we were foreign spies; they weren't exactly keen on giving us free information.

As I sat daydreaming, Hans tugged at my sleeve.

"Come on, let's go to breakfast," he suggested.

When we got to the kitchen there was a lukewarm bowl of week-old oatmeal waiting. It looked disgusting. But, it was the only food available so I wolfed it down. I said goodbye to Hans and rushed home to grab my books before I got on the bus. I had another day of tedious schoolwork in front of me, but I was unusually content. I was fifteen and could almost taste freedom.

I knew better than to be too optimistic, however. There had been numerous times when I thought the war must have been over already and pictured going back to Vienna. But the war was still happening and I was still stuck on this island. When we first got to Trinidad, I thought we would be back in Vienna within months. I knew life was bad there for us, but I thought the Nazi rule would pass rather quickly. I didn't expect it to result in a war, especially one this long. I wondered what the Germans had done to cause a war this long and horrible. My father and mother sometimes talked about the similarly long and horrible Great War that they said Germany also started.

I wondered a lot of things about life after the camp. Would Edith move back as well? Would we get our apartment and things back? What had happened to the store? It had been years since I sat in a presentable classroom. If it hadn't been for Mutti, I would be as stupid as a cow. I wanted my real life back. It seemed like everything normal had been stripped from me. Every time I adapted to a new situation, my world changed all over again.

Chapter 17:

Edith

Australia

Summer 1941

Life in Australia was not what I expected. My naive hopes of setting up a nice little family and continuing life as I had always known it were dashed by the realities of my new country and young adult life. With twenty years of life and three years of marriage under my belt, I can look back and laugh, but my first year with Hans in Australia was absolutely horrible.

We weren't truly in love with the each other, and the combination of everything else going on in our lives was too much for us to handle: moving across the world and leaving my parents, our experiences on the boat, living with his overbearing parents, our young age, and yes, of course, the baby.

Neither of us had expected the pregnancy and it scared both of us more than we were willing to admit. Hans' parents had tried to help with our relationship and my pregnancy, but there wasn't much they could do. Hans and I barely talked for six months and I spent every waking minute sitting by the door waiting for the mail to come to see if either of my parents had sent anything. I received letters from them every once and awhile but the letters came sparingly and I knew they hid the dark reality of their situation. I missed them so much and I was lonelier than an eighteen-year-old girl should be. I never left the house and had no friends.

My desperation was what caused it. Or, that is what the doctor told me after. I had woken up in the middle of the night sweating with my legs covered in blood. The pain pulsed through my abdomen and I screamed for help. Before the doctor could arrive, I had given birth three months early to a stillborn girl. I cannot even begin to describe the pain I felt in my heart after carrying my baby girl for months and then holding her dead body and burying her before I could even know her. I slipped even further into depression after that and stayed exclusively in my bedroom.

The doctor had informed me that I had lost the baby due to stress, depression, and the resulting fatigue. The pain was there for months and I'm not sure if Hans felt anything, but he started to talk to me more. After I had fully recovered physically we moved into a small flat closer to the city center of Melbourne. I started to go out more and joined an art group where I made friends closer to my age. I still felt a little ache for my loss but in a way I was grateful. I wasn't ready to be a mother yet and I had decided I didn't want to have a child until I was with my parents again. I needed to see my own mother again before I could become one myself.

My relationship with Hans felt like it had started over. Even though we lived together we began to go out on dates like lovebirds. He treated me like he was trying to win me again. I dare say we started to love each other. I truly enjoyed his company and liked our routine together. Even though I had my art friends, Hans became my best friend and the person I preferred to spend my time with. He made me laugh and we felt closer than we ever had been. He started to become interested in photography and we would go down to the coast together so he could take pictures and I could paint. For the first time I felt like I wanted to share things with someone else and tell them my secrets and my innermost thoughts. For two years life was pure bliss.

This morning Hans had an important meeting at his law firm so I was up early to make him breakfast and pour him a hot cup of coffee. I was planning on going to my art class after Hans left and then meet my new friend Diana for lunch. Then I was going to straighten up the flat and when Hans got home we were going out to dinner and dancing with another young couple from the law firm.

Hans walked out in his light lavender shirt and gray suit pants. He had matching grey suspenders and a tie which he was adjusting until it was just right. I had washed and pressed everything the night before and looked him up and down admiring both my work and my husband.

"Coffee!" Hans exclaimed, "And eggs!"

"It's an important day and I figured you needed a solid breakfast." I answered delighted at my domestic abilities.

"Thank you, dear. If all goes well today we may find ourselves closer to the beach in a year or two."

That was music to my ears. Hans and I both wanted to move towards the beach and out of the grimy inner city. I had even debated picking up a secretary shift or two.

I quickly reminded him as we he rushed out the door, "Remember, we have dinner with the Sterlings tonight!"

"Of course," he shouted with half a muffin in his mouth.

After he was out the door I started to get dressed myself. My wardrobe had adjusted to the warmer, more casual Australian environment and I slipped on a light, flowy blue blouse. I tucked it into a white skirt and slipped on a simple pair of flats. I wore my wedding pearls almost every day now and had a signature shade of red on my lips. I grabbed my art bag which was filled with my portfolio, pencils, paper, and paint plate. Fortunately, the studio provided extra paint for me which was a relief since it was rather expensive here.

I walked down our street feeling the same calm delight I felt almost every morning now. I waved to the friendly man who always sat at our corner and by the time I got to the class it was ten o'clock. I sat at my easel and began to set up. While I organized my station I listened in on the various conversations around the room. They were all about the war. They always were about the war. I hated hearing about the war. I hadn't heard from my parents since November 1939, two months into the war, and I figured the war was to blame for their lack of correspondence. I was scared that they might be in trouble or hurt and so I did not like thinking about the war. If I didn't think about the war, it was like it didn't even exist and in Australia, you didn't really notice the war. There was no fighting here and rationing didn't bother me because we didn't have money for extra food or luxuries anyways. Hans cared about the progress of the war and checked the papers every day but he hid them from me because he knew I didn't want to hear about it.

I watched as my classmates listened intently to the instructor and then proceeded to scrutinize a simple arrangement of fruit. The intense nature of some of the students never ceased to amuse me. After we started painting, the class passed rather quickly as it was a simple still-life tutorial. My teacher was eager to explore using a monochromatic pallet and constantly mentioned a Spanish artist named Picasso who was becoming prominent among the French and Spanish art crowds.

I left my class and went to meet Diana at a Jewish deli. I never imagined such a thing existed in Australia, but they were fairly popular here and Diana was obsessed with my Jewish heritage so she insisted we meet here. Diana reminded me slightly of my friend Liesl from back home and I fondly thought back on my lunch with Liesl at Demel's what felt like ages ago.

I entered the deli and noticed that the crowd seemed to be more somber than usual. I went to the counter and stupidly asked, "Did something happen?"

The man looked up with slightly red eyes and said, "Have you looked at the paper today?"

Oh god. It was something about the war. I should've just stopped there but at this point I was too curious.

I responded, "No. What is it?"

He handed me a paper and said, "It is really just a rumor but most of us have family or friends back in Europe who we are worried about."

I read the headline and gasped. I was horrified but I kept reading. I devoured the entire article and glanced at the crudely drawn picture at the bottom of the page. Angry at myself and the world, I slammed the newspaper down on the ground and put my hand against the wall to steady myself.

I asked the man, "Do you believe this?"

He said, "from what I saw, yes."

I thought about it and I realized what I had seen. I thought about the child saluting Hitler back in Vienna and the arrogance of the Nazis. I thought about Kristallnacht and our rushed departure from Vienna. Now it seemed Hitler was intent on killing hundreds of thousands of Jews. And yes, that could include my parents.

Diana walked in and rushed over to me.

I turned to Diana and softly said, "Let's reschedule," and ran out of the restaurant. I hurried home trying to block the tears from streaming down my face. My parents could be murdered any second now or they could already be dead. I thought about Ilse and Miriam sitting all alone and hungry in Vienna. I realized then that I had no idea where they were. My parents never mentioned my cousins in their letters. I wondered if that had already been taken away. Or maybe they had escaped. All I knew was that everyone at home was in imminent danger and I fell on my bed quaking in fear. Just like that, my life of bliss was over.

Chapter 18:

Miriam

Poland

Summer 1941

The forlorn whimpers of my mother and
aunt were still echoing through my head as I sat
with my back pressed against the hard train station
wall. We had been given a day to gather our things
and report to the Aspang Bahnhof and the news set
my parents on edge. I had silently packed up my
essential items with a small tear or two slipping out,
but I had no clue where we were going or what was
to come. It seemed that anything would be better
than the last few years cramped up and hungry in a
cold apartment.

Trains passed in and out of the station all
day as more people filled the terminal. Some people
arrived alone with only the clothes on their back
while others arrived with gaggles of children and
mountains of baggage. There were old men and
newborn babies and modern women and old rabbis.
It seemed almost every type of person in Vienna
was coming into the station. Except, they all had
one thing in common: they were all Jewish.

Of course because the Nazis had ordered us
here I figured this had something to do with us

being Jewish but it wasn't until I saw the sheer number of Jews gathered in one place that I was certain.

Between the summer heat and the masses of people, my clothes started sticking to my skin. Babies started to cry and children begged their parents for water. My mother was lying with her head on the pavement. I could not imagine sleeping through this noise and heat and I watched in awe as my mother calmly ignored the screams of a five year-old next to her.

After hours of waiting and observing the increasingly desperate crowd, our train pulled in. At first I paid no attention since it was a cattle train and dozens like it had already pulled in already. But as soon as the brakes stopped screeching, soldiers started barking orders and nudging people towards the trains. I shook my mother awake and looked around to make sure my aunt, uncle, and father were still next to me. We snatched up our suitcases and followed the rush of people onto the train. I held tight to my mother and aunt who were each holding fast to their husbands. We were all linked together and I was squeezing tight but I still checked behind me every couple seconds to make sure no one was lost. The crowd pushed and shoved and pressed hot, sticky bodies closer and closer together but our chain never broke.

We stumbled onto the ramp and into the train car. The heat hit me like a slap across the face. I had been hot in the station but the inside of the car was like an oven. The air was so thick I was having trouble breathing and as the soldiers slammed the door shut I could start to feel myself getting lightheaded. My mother was surprisingly alert although Aunt Charlotte looked rather faint. I tried to push myself towards a wall so I could lean against something but the car was packed so tight I could barely move or turn around.

The train lurched forward causing a few people to almost fall over. This caused a whole wave of people to lose their balance and the whole back row of the car slammed against the back wall creating the disgusting sound of skin and bone smacking against wood. It became clear just how worse life could get.

Smothered against the rows and rows of other sweaty bodies, I thought back on the past three years since Ilse left. I could not believe it had been that long since I last saw my cousin. I had no clue where she was or if she was safe or if she had even made it to Trinidad at all. A few months after she left for Amsterdam we heard that Hitler had taken Holland as well. I spent many hours worrying about how vulnerable Ilse could have been in whether in open seas or stuck in Amsterdam.

Since Ilse left, I was forced to grow up a lot. I was only fifteen but I felt much older. When Edith was seventeen she was barely responsible for anything at all except the occasional chore. Being the only child in a starving household almost forced me to have responsibilities equal to those of my parents. I also had to take care of my mother. My mother had been weak and depressed for years and being cooped up in that apartment only made her worse. I tried to cheer up my mother by reading or drawing for her but it seemed to have little effect. I hadn't seen the glimpse of a smile since I was eleven years old.

A scream on the train snapped me back to reality. A young woman was crying hysterically while someone else groaned in pain. I tried to look over people to catch a glimpse of what was going on.

"Mein Gott!" my aunt gasped.

"What happened Aunt Charlotte?" I whispered.

"It looks like an old woman has fainted and is--"

"What?" I asked a little louder.

"She's been crushed."

I looked again. I didn't even understand how someone could be crushed but then I saw through the various legs and skirts, a woman underneath people's feet. She wasn't moving. She was dead.

A little girl next to me tugged her mother's skirt and asked, "Mama why would they kill that woman?"

The mother looked down at her daughter and said, "Darling, they didn't try to but there's no room on the train. It was an accident."

The little girl stared at the woman's body, fascinated by her first taste of cruelty.

After what seemed like hours on the train, the heat began to subside and the light began to fade from the cracks in the cattle car. I guess it was nighttime but after that old woman's death, I don't think anyone else was planning on sleeping. Aunt Charlotte leaned into Uncle Hugo's arms and whispered, "I miss our daughter."

My uncle replied, "Me too. Me too." He then let out a couple of coughs to cover the tears building up.

After light began to seep back through the cracks, the train abruptly stopped causing another wave of panic. I didn't know where we were but I heard the familiar nasty shrieks of Nazis and the bark of dogs. Four boot stomps came up our ramp and the car door was flung ajar. The light was blinding and I couldn't open my eyes at first.

People started shuffling out of the car immediately. I slowly moved towards the door. I didn't know why but I was extremely nervous. I got closer and closer to the door and saw what seemed like a giant prison. There were soldiers and guard towers everywhere and a wide expanse of dirt and shacks. As I walked out the door I turned back and gave a smile to my family.

A guard grabbed my shoulder and yanked me out of my mother's grasp. He put the butt of his gun into the small of my back and pushed me towards a group on the side. Another guard addressed him and said, "skinny, weak, and young."

He looked at my mother and said, "frail. Looks dead already."

My aunt, father, and uncle were all addressed as, "a little too old. Too bad for them."

Another guard grabbed the bag out of my hand, threw it in a pile and pushed me further along.

In my mind I was screaming at this guards. I wanted to yell, "why are you doing this to me? Don't touch me like that! Don't take my stuff! When will I get it back? Why are you talking about me and my family like that?" Fear kept me silent.

As a guard took my mother's bag she began to cry and clutched my father's arm. Aunt Charlotte was whispering to Uncle Hugo about Edith and she let out a few prayers. A guard stopped us and a large group began to gather. I looked to my left and saw two other large groups: one with men and another with women and children.

A soldier addressed our group. He screamed, "You are going to take a shower. Please step into the changing rooms and undress. Remember where you put your clothes so you can get that back later."

Some people started panicking and crying even more. I didn't understand; a shower sounded nice to me after our sweaty train ride. A few couples embraced and mothers kissed their children's foreheads. Others looked around seeming just as confused as I was.

I gazed at the building we were supposed to shower in. Little white flakes were billowing out of the chimney and covering the surrounding area in a gray blanket. I didn't know what they were burning but the scene sent shivers down my spine.

As I walked towards the building I looked around me taking in the pure blue of the vibrant sky and the crunch of the dirt and the smell of the crisp morning air. I looked at a bluebird flying overhead and a patch of green grass growing near the train tracks. I lifted my hand and felt the wind rush through my fingers and my hair. I didn't know what was going on or what was going to happen, but I needed to take everything in before I entered that building. I stepped in the doorway and turned around. My mother grabbed my hand and gave me a soft smile, the first I had seen in years. My father let a tear slip out and kissed the top of my head. And that was all.

Chapter 19:

Ilse

Trinidad

Spring 1943

"I'm sorry but I just don't feel that way about you anymore," I said to Hans as he stood at my doorstep sulking.

"But Ilse! I don't understand!" He retorted.

"I'm sorry Hans, but I've moved on."

Hans struggled for a response for a few seconds and then turned and stomped away. I felt bad for him, but ever since we had been released from the camp, I just didn't want to be with him anymore. I had learned about all the fun things life had to offer and Hans was just a little… boring.

Once the authorities decided we were "clean" and not spies they let us go back to our normal lives. Some families really were going back to their daily lives, but my family still felt like newcomers. While that was sad at times, it also meant that there were still a ton of things to discover on the island. I got ice cream and went dancing with my new friends from school. I played at the beach and explored the coast with George. Occasionally, I worked with Mutti and Papa at the new store they had opened up.

The best part was that the war had brought tons of handsome young soldiers to the island. Whenever my friends and I went to do something we would run into a group of soldiers willing to buy us some food or take us to one of the USO dances.

So yes, I felt bad for Hans, but the breakup really didn't affect me too much. In fact, as he walked away, I began to get ready to meet Susie, one of my new friends. She was from the United States and her father worked in the military as a high-level communications officer. We met one day at my parents' store while she shopped for a birthday present for her mother. I hated that we didn't go to school together but she was at an international school down the road that was mainly for Americans. I, on the other hand, had to struggle in the dusty, humid rooms of the state school. We wore uniforms and mainly spoke English, but it was generally filthy and unsophisticated. The girls there didn't like me either. I was the only Jewish girl and they all thought I was foreign and strange.

My classmate Cassandra hated me the most and regularly taunted me saying, "You think you're white and all but really I know you aren't white. You're Jewish." She would then run around chanting *Ilse the Jew, Ilse the Jew* in a singsong voice. I hated her.

Susie was different though. She didn't care that I was Jewish at all. When I asked her if it ever bothered he she nonchalantly said, "No, I know a ton of Jews. Back in New York, my doctor is

Jewish and so is my dad's lawyer. Oh and there was a Jewish boy in my class. Oh and a Jewish man next door! Yeah, back home there were a lot of Jews."

I was very excited to go see Susie today because I had yet to fill her in on the past week of school and tell her that I finally broke up with Hans. Walking out the door, I swiped on a little lipstick (Mutti let me wear that now) and grabbed a light blue sweater.

I shouted, "Bye Mutti! I'm going to meet Susie now! Love you!"

She shouted back, "No yelling through the house. I love you too!"

I slammed the door behind me and as I walked away I heard Mutti yell again, "don't slam the door!"

I met Susie at the park where we sat down on a bench and started filling each other in on every single detail of the past week. I told her about Cassandra falling in the mud in front of the whole class and about how sad Hans looked when I broke up with him. She reenacted one of her father's angry rants about the stubbornness of the British and shared gossip about her friends back in America.

As we chatted excitedly, two young soldiers watched us from afar and nervously paced around our area. They exchanged glances until finally one came up and said, "My friend and I noticed you two sitting over here and since we're on our lunch break…uh…we were wondering if you might get something to eat with us." He nodded at Susie and said, "Your father's Commander Emerson, right?"

Susie turned a bright shade of red and nodded. She looked at me and then looked at the soldier and then looked back at me and then looked at the soldier again and said, "We would love to join you for lunch!"

I interrupted, rather stunned that we were going to lunch with two strangers, and asked, "What are your names?"

He responded, "Oh of course, my bad. I'm Robert Sharp and that over there is Martin Angove." He waved over to Martin and beckoned him to come join us.

Martin was obviously the better looking of the two but he looked a bit cold and distant. I shyly smiled and said, "I'm Ilse, it's a pleasure"

He awkwardly responded, "Marty, the pleasure is mine."

The other soldier chimed in, "Oh yeah, call him Marty and you can call me Bob."

Susie and I linked arms and followed Marty and Bob to Cliff's, a nearby cafe where soldiers frequently took lunch breaks. Susie and Bob hit it off immediately which left me to entertain Marty. At first he seemed rather firm and awkward but I soon realized he had a sweet spot and we had many things in common. He told me about his Jewish family in the Bronx and how he was serving to help the Jews of Europe, which seemed noble. He had a rather strange sense of humor but I liked it and genuinely laughed as his odd jokes. At the end of lunch, right as I was leaving, he started to turn red. He stepped closer to me and started to say, "Um, Ilse, I really enjoyed lunch and actually there's this USO dance coming up--" *Oh yes! A dance!* "-- and I was wondering if you would come with me?"

Well, that was all it took to win me over. As Susie and I walked home I excitedly began to consider which of the dresses in my closet I would wear for the dance.

~

Marty looped his hand around my waist and twirled me across the dance floor as I giggled with glee. We were at another USO dance, our seventh so far, and I was happier than ever. The past seven months had been tremendous fun and although Susie and Bob broke up after 2 months, it was nice having a close circle of friends. I had graduated from the group of girls who just flirted with the soldiers and moved up to the girls who were going steady with their soldiers and I liked being in that latter group. I gained even more friends and got invited to all sorts of events.

At the dance, Marty and I danced and laughed, but I noticed that he seemed more nervous than usual. He was sweating, which could be explained by the dancing, but he also kept wringing his hands and scratching his head. I couldn't figure out why he was so nervous. My first theory was that he had something important to do tomorrow or that one of his commanding officers was in the room. I looked around but failed to notice anyone important-looking.

I asked him, "What's going on with you? You seem nervous."

This just made him more nervous and he scrambled to say, "Nothing. I'm fine; it's just very hot in here. I'm going to go outside."

With that he turned and walked outside lighting a cigarette as he hurried away. I wrinkled my nose in disgust. I had tried a cigarette once before at Susie's behest, but hated them. I wanted to like them as almost everyone smoked and it was such an elegant thing, but they just made me want to throw up. I hated when Marty smoked and the smell clung to his jacket.

I walked over to Susie and asked her, "Have you noticed that Marty is acting weird?"

She bit her lip and tried not to smile, "Just be patient with him. I'm sure he's nervous for a good reason."

I had no clue what she was talking about and went outside to check on Marty and his nerves. As soon as he saw me he threw his cigarette on the ground and stomped it out.

"Um, Ilse, I wanted to ask you something very important. I've already talked to your father and everything," He stammered.

"Ok… What is it?" I responded curiously.

"Well, it has been seven months and I think you are just great, just really really great. I know you're a little young and, well, I'm still in the navy, but I can make a good life for us, I promise."

I gasped.

"So Ilse, will you do me the honor of being my wife?"

I almost spilled my drink.

A wife! Marty's wife! Wow. I really liked him and he was American so I could move to the US. He told me he had a nice Jewish family and he is very handsome and so, "yes!" I responded without thinking any further. "Of course."

~

I was just beginning to notice the signs of a bump, but my body was definitely feeling the baby. I was constantly sick and felt heavier than ever.

Mutti was frantic both because of my impending departure and because of the pregnancy.

Marty had been overjoyed when he heard and prayed every night for a boy, which he planned to name Martin. I didn't tell him but I wanted a girl. A baby girl would keep me company in America amongst all the strangers.

I folded the last of my skirts and snapped the suitcase closed. I was leaving home again although this time I was headed off somewhere better. I was going to America to become a citizen and create a safe and happy life for my baby. I was excited to fly to New York and live with Marty's parents but I just wish I didn't have to leave my dear Mutti and Papa.

Mutti and I left for the airport and Marty met us there. I had only been married a few months and I was already leaving him. It wasn't right to say, but I didn't think I would miss Marty as much as Mutti. Nonetheless, I was grateful to see him one last time.

I looked up at Mutti with tears in my eyes and said, "I will see you soon, I promise. I'll bring you over as soon as I can."

She pulled me into her chest and said, "Don't worry about me. Focus on yourself and the baby. I love you forever."

As she held me I was reminded of leaving Vienna all those years ago. I remembered saying goodbye to Edith and then to Miriam and I realized how it must have felt for Edith to leave with Hans: heartbreaking yet hopeful.

Mutti let go of me and blew me a kiss. I started walking away and almost pulled her along with me as I tried to keep hold of her hand. But then I dropped it and looked forward towards the Trinidad sunset and the little plane. I held my hand over my swollen stomach and stepped into the cabin.

Chapter 20:

Ilse

Australia

Fall 1950

I kissed both my little girls on the tops of their heads and promised I'd be back before they even noticed I was gone.

Tina toddled towards me and gave me a toothy grin. She was still little and smiled at everything. Judy was less pleased and stomped in front of her little sister. She gave me a firm, "I don't want you to leave. Why can't just Daddy go?"

I laughed and reassured her, "This is a trip for Mommy and Daddy but your Mutti and Opapa will take good care of you. You'll have so much fun in San Diego!"

I loved my daughters and of course I didn't want to leave them, but their pleas couldn't sway me. I was so excited to be reunited with Edith. She and I had found each other after the war and had written to each other fairly regularly, but I hadn't seen her since I was twelve. When Marty and I found a brochure for a cruise to Australia I begged him to go so we could see Edith and Hans. I was dying to see my cousin. But, I also had to tell her the details about Miriam and her parents. She didn't know everything yet.

~

Sydney Harbor was gorgeous. Birds fluttered overheard and the city skyline stood out with sophisticated skyscrapers. The sun shone down on everything, a pleasant change from our chilly winter in Bridgeport. I wondered if this was how Edith felt when she arrived from Vienna.

The plan was for Edith and Hans to pick us up in Sydney and then drive to Melbourne where we would stay the night and meet the cruise ship the next morning. I grabbed Marty's hand and kissed him lightly. Marty and I had had a rough few months and I was hoping the trip would be good for us as well. When Marty first got back from the war, our family was incredibly happy. Judy was still a baby and we had Tina soon after. But now it had been more than five years since Marty's return and he was becoming increasingly unhappy at work and then at home. We had actually debated moving away from Connecticut and finding a place near my parents in Southern California. Marty had a dream of owning a beautiful house in Beverly Hills surrounded by palm trees and sun.

As we waited at the dock for Edith and Hans to pick us up, my heart started to pound. I was nervous to see Edith. In my mind she was still my seventeen year old idol and though I had thought about her and Miriam consistently since I left Vienna, she was basically a stranger to me. Would it be awkward? Would we still feel connected? Would she look the same? I certainly didn't look like the round-faced short-haired cherub I used to be.

A tiny little red car pulled up and a woman got out. She had dark hair tied up and a pale face with a smudge of red lipstick over her lips. There were a few fine lines on her forehead and her face seemed slimmer than I remember, but I knew in an instant that this was my Edith. She seemed to study me in the same way and when had finished and made tearful eye contact, we ran and embraced each other.

"Oh Ilse!" She cried and tears began to flow.

"Edith… I can't believe it's really you," I said as I too began to cry.

She was still so sophisticated and glamorous and she still felt like my childhood role model even though our age difference seemed minor at this point. Marty was older than Edith.

We all piled into her small red car, one reunited family, and drove towards Melbourne.

~

Edith's home was lovely and cozy. It was in a nice suburb of Melbourne and reminded me of my parents' neighborhood in San Diego. Marty and I were sleeping in a beautiful guest room on the second floor that was decorated with seashells and pictures of the ocean. Edith and Hans had a gorgeous room with a view of their garden out back.

After Edith and Hans showed us around and Marty and I got settled, we all sat down in the living room and began to reflect on the past. The majority of the memories were shared between Edith and me but Hans remembered quite a few of them and reflected on his own time in Vienna. Marty just sat in silence and observed us, fascinated with the life I had before I met him.

As we laughed and cried about our times back in Austria, I thought it would be as good a time as any to tell Edith.

I nervously started, "I didn't tell you this because, well, this isn't the kind of thing you tell someone in a letter, but I know what happened to Miriam and your parents and Aunt Berta and Uncle Joseph."

"Stop. I don't want to know." She firmly interrupted.

I was shocked and retorted, "What do you mean? You have to know! It's our family!"

She took a breath and then explained, "I don't want to think about that horrible time or those horrible people and if they ended up in those horrible camps, I don't want to think about those either."

"Edith... "

"Look Ilse, have you ever wondered why I never went back to Vienna or why I never had children? Vienna is an evil place where the people of Austria let something like the Holocaust happen. It is a painful place with too many terrible memories. And with children... it was a decision I made after my miscarriage during the war. I decided, and Hans agreed with me, that we didn't want to bring children into this evil and cruel world. After what happened to our family and what people of this earth let happen to the Jews, I could not imagine bringing another life onto this planet."

I could not understand what she was saying. After everything we had gone through, she didn't realize the joy in every day? I felt so lucky to be alive and I wanted to remember my family and know about my family and make a great life for my children, but she didn't want any of that. She just wanted to forget. I came away from the horrors of the Holocaust embracing everyday and seeing how beautiful the world could be. From what I could tell, she just came away seeing the evils of the world.

"Edith, I know it hurts to remember and think about our family and their suffering, but it's our history and it's important. I traveled to Israel and went to the Holocaust records to ask about our family," I started to explain.

Hans put his arm around Edith and she hung her head, "Go on."

"Well, they don't have any records of our family, but they are positive that our family was taken to a concentration camp. Because there is no record of our family, they can assume our family was taken to Auschwitz-Birkenau, the only camp that didn't record people when they sent them straight to the gas chambers."

Edith cried out as if she had just been stabbed. She buried her head in Hans' arms and shook as she sobbed. I started to cry as well. It felt like yesterday that Miriam and I had skipped hand in hand through Vienna and I couldn't imagine what it felt like for Edith to learn about her parent's horrible death.

I walked over to Edith and wrapped my arms around her. We held each other, remembering our families and our cousin, our old home, and the ruin of the Holocaust.

Author's Notes
(AKA the complete true story)

My great grandma, who I call Grams, was born in Vienna, Austria on May 11, 1927. She is the character Ilse and all of Ilse's scenes and experiences come from what Grams has told me about her life.

Edith is also a real person. She was my great grandmother's cousin and did indeed elope and move to Australia. While she is no longer alive, my great grandmother shared what she remembers about Edith. I used those memories to build Edith as a person and to shape her scenes. While much about Edith's life in Australia is unknown, there are a few things that are true and important. Firstly, Edith and Hans never had children. While the miscarriage scene was created out of my imagination, they truly never had children for the reasons Edith expresses in the book. Also, the scenes in Chapter 20 are real. My great grandmother and great grandfather did meet Edith and Hans in Vienna and had a touching conversation very similar to the one in the book. Finally, regarding Edith, she and Hans surprisingly never got divorced and had a long and happy marriage. Even after rushing to marry at such a young age under traumatic circumstances, Edith and Hans loved each other until the end.

Miriam is a character developed out of several real figures. My great grandmother's memory of her time in Vienna is limited as she was a child but over the years she has recalled memories of Jewish friends and family who lived outside the Ringstrasse. She vividly remembers an aunt and uncle who never had children and were poorer than the rest of the family. Miriam is primarily based off of that aunt. Her stories and experiences also come from small details my great grandmother has remembered about certain friends and a good deal of research on Jews in Vienna.

Miriam's death is a difficult part of this book but it is also an integral part. It shows the fate of so many Jews and the fate of most of my family. While Ilse and Edith escaped the worst of the Holocaust, most of their family including all other aunts and uncles and Edith's parents, perished in Auschwitz. After visiting Holocaust databases in Jerusalem, Paris, Vienna, Berlin, and those on the

Internet, there is no record of my family. Experts have told us this is a sign that they were sent directly to the gas chambers at Auschwitz-Birkenau. We know this because the lack of records only occurred at Auschwitz where they would immediately send people to gas chambers. In other camps they recorded your information even if sending you to your death and for certain people at Auschwitz, they recorded your information if you were to stay and work. Miriam's death is tragic, but it is true and representative of my family and the 6 million other Jews of the Holocaust. This was not fake or exaggerated. This was a real phenomenon carried out by a legal and supported government. It was democratic and it was horrible beyond words. Let us remember this as we face any and every government.

Now as far as the rest of Ilse's story, it ends with me and my sister. It starts with Mutti who I never got to meet but admire nonetheless. I still carry her name, Regine.

After Ilse left for the United States, she gave birth to my Great Aunt Judy (later changed to Judi). After, when Marty came back from the war she gave birth to my grandma, Tina. While Ilse first settled in the Bronx, her and Marty soon moved to Bridgeport, Connecticut. When Ilse turned 21, she was able to bring her parents to America and they moved from Trinidad to San Diego. Ilse and Marty didn't always have the best marriage and although she seldom admits it, he would be, in today's terms, considered abusive. But to her, a survivor of the world's greatest horrors, this was just normal. She also nonchalantly refers to herself as a "war bride." After the rest of Ilse's family came to California, Ilse and Marty moved to Los Angeles. They even reached Marty's great dream of living in Beverly Hills.

In the midst of this 1950s American life, Tina and Judi grew up and married and had children, one of which was my mother. Unfortunately Judi didn't have long left. Marty's family carried the BRCA gene, common in Ashkenazi Jews, which gives females a high chance of contracting breast, uterine, or ovarian cancer.

Judi passed away from breast cancer at 37 years old. My great grandfather Marty also passed away from a heart attack at age 60. And finally,

Tina, my beloved grandmother who I miss every day, passed away in 2015 from an eight year battle with ovarian and uterine cancer as a result of the BRCA gene. Ilse's parents also passed away: Mutti of pancreatic cancer and Papa of a broken heart. George, however, is still alive and lives in the bay area of California.

Ilse, my Grams, the strongest woman I have ever met, survived the Holocaust and had to bury her husband and both her children. She nevertheless remains steadfast in her optimistic view of life. Today she lives down the street from me overlooking the ocean in beautiful La Jolla, California. I see her at least once a week and her smile never fails to solve the latest problems of being a teenager. I love her more than I could ever describe. She is the unceasing light of my life. I hope you have come to love her in a small way too.

- Isabelle Regine Kenagy

Thank You

I'd like to thank a few people who made this book possible. Of course Grams, the center of this story whose favorite character is herself. Thank you for telling me your story and for teaching me all you know. My parents have also dedicated a lot to this project and kept me motivated to finish this book even in the midst of SATs and finals and teenage angst. This book would have never been possible without Mr. Mathew Valji who is an expert on the Holocaust and a wonderful teacher and mentor. You kept me on track and historically accurate. You give so much to your students and are a true example of what a teacher with passion can do for their students. Mr. Gary Hendrickson and Ms. Amy Allen also deserve their fair share of credit for teaching me how to write. H, you gave me the soul and passion and Ms. Allen, you taught me grit and the ladder of abstraction. Also, of course, my baby sister Chiara recorded an audio version of the book, which may seem small but was the only way Grams, who at 91 only suffers from poor eyesight, could access this book. Finally, Lisa Alexander did all the wonderful artwork for this book. Her creative masterpieces pulled this collection of chapters together and made it into a book. Thank you for dedicating your time, even though you didn't have to, to help make one of my dreams possible. You are so talented. Thank you to Sonia Gaiane, John Stein, and all the other people I forced to read and edit this book. I love all of you for what you have given me and motivated me to do. You all made this possible.

Ilse Schlesinger – December 1938

Mein Papperle
bei der Abfahrt
aus dem Hitlerreich

Dezember 1938
in Wien

Made in the USA
San Bernardino, CA
03 January 2019